DON'T PLAY IF YOU CAN'T PAY

DON'T PLAY IF YOU CAN'T PAY

WRITTEN BY:
SHARYN PAIGE

ANGEL GIRL PUBLISHING
NEW YORK, NEW YORK

DEDICATION

This book is dedicated to the following people:

All the Youth and Young Adults at E.W.B.C.

Ethan, Brieanna, Brittney, Kaisson, Autumn, Travis, Daniel, Alyson and my little Diva "Symora"

Acknowledgements

First and Foremost, I must give Honor to my Lord and Savior Jesus Christ. "I Can Do All Things Through Christ Which Strengthens Me". (Philippians 4:13)

Special Thank you to my Pastor: The Esteemed Rev. Dr. Sean P. Gardner, Sr; for always encouraging me, I truly appreciate you.

To my God-Daughters Brieanna and Brittney, I am so proud of you guys, you are my heart.

Daniel: God-mommy has not forgotten you, now we can spend time together, lol.

To my Youth and Young Adults at East Ward Missionary Baptist Church, I love you all so immensely. You guys are the best.

To Alvin (AJ) Jackson, thank you for always making me smile at the right time.

To these special ladies (my angels): Words cannot express the love that I have for each of you: Tye, Mona, Barbara, Gwen H. Norma, Mega, Jennifer, Shareen, Denise F., Kioka, Sis Anna.

Daren, a girl couldn't ask for a better friend/brother.

Terrence thanks for your unconditional love and support. Love You Much.

Joyce, Stephanie, Tracey, Nicole, Travis and Autumn you guys have been a true blessing in my life.

And of course my B.F.F. Mia I am so glad that you are in my life, I love you more than you know.

Tylie, Yolanda, Rasheedah, Jimmy, Iris C. (Diva), Angelina, Lizette, Ebony, Amanda, Monique, Teresa, Tasha, Chante, Damaris, for all the support you have given me, I am truly grateful for all of you. This is Your Season to Reap What You've Sown.

To my nephews: Ethan, Kaisson, you two are my heart, love you both always. My nieces Ashlee, Jessica, PJ, Love you.

Patricia much love, I appreciate you, (Am I Grown Now), lol…. Lashaunda, thank you for always making my hair look good.

My Eastward Family, thank you.

To my cousin Lina Poo, stay sweet and beautiful as always.

To Michelle, the best tax person in the world: God's got a blessing with your name on it.

To my P.I.C. Nhjela a.k.a Nadia, thanks for the wonderful sistership. I appreciate you always.

To my Memphis Sister Ronnie, Love You Chick.

Jamal, I am so proud of you, God has greater things in store for you.

Sean you are definitely one-of-a-kind, I'm so glad you're in my life.

My handsome cousins, Eric and Wadius, you guys are the best.

And to anyone that I have forgotten, charge it to my head and not to my heart.

CHAPTER ONE

It's about three thirty, on a warm summer Saturday afternoon. Vanessa is at her home in East Hampton, New York. Her best friend Vikki decides to stop by the house. Vanessa answers the door she is not her usual fun-loving self.

Vikki notices that Vanessa is crying. "Girl what's wrong? Let's go in the living room and talk about it."

"Oh Vikki it's nothing important, it's just that I have PMS (Pre-Man Syndrome)."

"Wooo! Girl, please don't scare me like that, the way you were crying and moping around here I thought that something was seriously wrong. By the way how is Tyrone doing?"

Vanessa says sarcastically to Vikki, "He is getting on my reserve nerve. I try to talk to him but he never has any time for me; and since he's gotten more contracts he hardly spends any time at home. All he does is sleep and pee."

"What! Now Vanessa you know you're wrong, you should be glad that you have a man who is working and taking care of the home."

"Vikki, that's the problem. He's taking care of the home but he is forgetting about me, and he seems distant when I talk about adopting children. He thinks that his first child should not belong to a previous owner.

Have you ever heard of such nonsense?"

"Vanessa, you need to be patient with Tyrone. He will eventually come around to the fact that adoption might be the only way to go for the two of you to have children.   I'm going to trust and pray that GOD changes your situation around and that you will be able to have children naturally."

"Vikki, maybe you're right, but it will take a sho nuff miracle for him to change his mind. I'm almost scared to tell him that I want to go back to school and finish getting my degree; he is not going to go for it."

"Vanessa, you need to tell Tyrone 'to build a bridge and get over it'; you have to do what's best for you."

"Vikki, you try telling Tyrone that. He thinks I should be at home cooking and cleaning, and satisfying his needs."

"Vanessa, I know what will get your mind off things."

"And what is that Vikki?"

"Let's go shopping and spend some money."

"Girl you ain't said nothing but a word; give me a minute while I get dressed."

"Vanessa girl, are you ready yet? Let's go, I want to get to the stores before they run out of things."

"I'm coming, give me a minute."

"Vanessa, you have exactly one minute, fifty-nine seconds, fifty-eight, fifty-seven seconds! Girl you are the slowest."

"Here I am girl, now you know when it comes to spending money, I'm the best at it. Let's go so I can be back by the time Tyrone gets home from work."

Tyrone walks through the door and, as usual, expects his wife to be at his beck and call. "Vanessa, Vanessa baby are you home?" *Where is that woman? She hasn't been home lately and I don't like it; we will have a discussion about this later.*

Vanessa finally arrives at home, she is in a good mood because she has found a lot of nice things. "Hi honey, how are you? How was your day at the office?"

Tyrone is heated. "I am fine! And my day was busy as usual. Never mind that, where were you?"

"I was shopping, duh!!! Do you think I have all these packages in my arms to look pretty?"

"Look woman, I don't have time for your smart-ass answers; you've been out spending money on yourself again, and of course you didn't think about me did you?"

"By the way Tyrone, I bought a couple of things for you too."

"Honey I'm sorry, please forgive me. I've had a rough day at work, let me see what I got. Wow you got me the Rolex that I wanted; it's not my birthday or anything like that. Okay what's up?"

What do you mean 'what's up?' Can't I do something nice for my man? Geez."

"I don't have a problem with you doing something nice for me, but I know you woman," Tyrone says with a smirk." One gift is something nice, but four gifts means you want something, or something is on your mind… so what is it?"

"Tyrone, that's a shame that you would think I want something."

"Okay Vanessa, I'm going to ask you for the last time, 'what is it'?"

"Well I do want something. Well, umm how do I say this?"

"Will you just spit it out woman!"

"I want to go back to school to finish my degree and I want to work more hours. I can get a promotion at work, and I will be able to work on a full time basis, instead of part-time."

"It's out of the question, Vanessa."

"What do you mean, 'it's out of the question? Tyrone, won't you even hear me out?"

"I said no, and that's the end of the conversation."

"Tyrone, until you can give me a good reason why I can't go back to school, I am going back to school."

"Look woman I am your husband and I said you're not going back. It is what it is. No school and no more hours, you should be happy that I am allowing you to work the hours that you are working now. Give it up, end of discussion." Vanessa is trying to get in the last word. Tyrone is ignoring her; he is answering his cell phone. "Hello how are you doing today?"

"Tyrone whoever that is; tell them they need to call you back so we can finish this conversation!"

"Excuse me for a moment. Vanessa can't you see that I am on the phone, and for the last time we are not having this discussion. I said no and that's my final answer; this conversation is over, end of discussion."

"Tyrone Tyler, you make me so sick; this is ridiculous that you are acting so childish. I'm going upstairs. And for the record I am going to school. one way or another. Oh! I could kill you right now."

Vanessa calls Vikki, but when Vikki answers she barely recognizes Vanessa voice. "Hello who is this?"

"Hey girl it's only your best friend Vanessa, how are you?"

"Vanessa, it doesn't sound like you at all. Are you okay?   I can hear something strange in your voice, do you need me to come over there?"

"It's Tyrone, can you believe that he said that he doesn't want me to go back to school to finish my degree and he said that I can't work longer hours."

"What! Did you ask him why not? You need to press him on that.   I don't understand why he wouldn't, in all the years I have known Tyrone, he seems like a pretty reasonable guy. Isn't he the one who always talks about education? And now for him to tell you that you can't go back to finish your degree, it just seems a little weird to me."

"Girl I did ask him about it he said no; and just when I thought that he was going to give me a legitimate answer, he decided to take a call on his cell. I'm getting sick of him."

"Girl calm down; here's what I want you to do, get dressed and come over here so that we can talk rationally."

"I can't come over there now, there is no way that he is going to let me leave."

"What! Is he your father? You're a grown woman, girl I'll be waiting."

"You know what, you are right! Who does he think he is? He is not my father! I will be there soon let me change my clothes." Vanessa is coming down stairs; she notices Tyrone in the living room on the couch snoring like a Cheshire cat, as usual. She realizes that this is a good time for her to leave so she tries and sneaks past him.

"Going somewhere, are we?"

How in the hell did he hear or see me? I was quiet as a button. "Yes, I was just going over to Vikki's house!"

"You're going to Vikki's house for what, at this time of the night?"

"Just to talk, that's all, nothing else."

"I don't think so, I'm hungry you haven't cooked a thing and you want to go and chit chat with your girlfriend. Not tonight you won't, and don't make faces behind my back."

"Yes master butthole!"

"Vanessa, what did you call me?"

Mumbling under her breathe she says, "You really don't want to know. Nothing darling, Tyrone you are getting on my last nerve, I can't take it anymore"…

"Vikki, I had to call you."

"Vanessa where are you?   I have been waiting for over one hour for you; it only takes ten minutes to get from your house to my house."

"Of course you know Tyrone won't let me leave the house. I don't know what I'm going to do anymore, I'm at wits end."

"Maybe you guys need to go to counseling."

"Wrong answer. Tyrone would never go for that, you really want problems for me. I will be divorced for sure.   Well let me go. I just need to think right now, I don't want to do the wrong thing, (ttyl) girl; and Vikki, before you ask 'what a ttyl is,' it means talk to you later. Love you girl, gotta go now."

Vanessa has changed into something more comfortable, she is about to come back downstairs to cook dinner for Tyrone. As she walks by he grabs her by the arm and pulls her close to him. In his deep apologetic voice, he says to his wife, "Baby I am so sorry for talking to you in such a nasty manner. I have a lot going on at work, and of course I took it out on the person closest to me. And you know that you can hang out with Vikki anytime that you want."

"It's alright, I'm going to fix your dinner now." As she tries to pull away from him, Tyrone pulls her closer to him and kisses her.

She still isn't happy. She is quiet at dinner and too scared to say anything to Tyrone, fearing he will go off on her again.

"Baby is there something wrong? You are very quiet."

"Tyrone I'm okay."

"Vanessa Tyler, we have been married long enough for me to know that there is something wrong, now what is it?"

"Trust me, there is nothing wrong.   Everything will be alright."

Tyrone gets up from the table and walks over to Vanessa. He takes her by the hand and pulls her up. "Baby, I want you to know that I love you so very much, and you can talk to me about anything."

Crying through her tears, she tells Tyrone, "Well, I don't think that I make you happy anymore, and I'm sorry that I haven't been able to give you what you want. Tyrone I was thinking, maybe it would be a good idea if we separated for a while."

"Woman, what in the world are you talking about? I was happy with you when I first married you, and I'm happy now, is this really what's bothering you? What are you hiding from me? What do you mean you haven't been able to give me what I want?"

"Tyrone, you know as well as I do that you want children, and I haven't been able to give you any."

"And so this is why you think we should separate? Now I'm really hurt."

"Tyrone, I'm sorry, but I'm entitled to my feelings, and that's what's bothering me."

Tyrone is thinking to himself; deep down inside he does want children, but he wouldn't dare tell Vanessa that this is the missing piece to true happiness in their marriage. "Baby let's not go there again with that, I'm okay with it, and who knows maybe one day things will change. In the meantime, I love you; and don't worry about not having kids, everything will happen in God's time. Now let's go upstairs and go to sleep. I have to get up for work very early in the morning. Baby, I'm sorry I have to take this call. Go ahead I will meet you in our room in a minute."

Tyrone's mistress in on the phone. "Hey handsome, I just called to say good night and that I love you."

Tyrone can't say I love you to Kayla on the phone because his wife is in the house with him, and he is afraid she might hear him. "Okay thank you so much." He is trying to play it off. "The meeting has been re-scheduled for eight o'clock tomorrow morning and not ten o'clock, okay thank you, and you have a good night as well."

CHAPTER TWO

"Good morning, how is my handsome husband doing? Tyrone, you are bright eyed and rearing to go this morning."

"Vanessa, I can't believe that you are up this early. Are you sick or something? Honey it's nothing like that at all. The office asked me to come in a little earlier today I have a lot of work to do."

"Well, what time are you getting home?"

"Tyrone I don't know, I told you yesterday that the firm wants me to work more hours and I told them that I would; this could lead to full-time employment for me. I am really excited about working the extra hours."

Well, you need to tell them that you can't work longer hours because you need to be home taking care of the house."

"Tyrone it's too early in the morning, and I'm not having this discussion with you. I will be home late and that's final."

"Oh really Vanessa, we will see about that! I expect you home by six o'clock."

"Oh really! I will talk to you later honey. I cannot and will not be late for work."

"Vanessa I hope you heard what I said!"

"Whatever Tyrone!"

"Vanessa please do not "Whatever" me. I mean six o'clock, or I will come to your office and escort you home personally. Vanessa I mean it, six o'clock sharp, not six o'clock and one second. Please don't test me."

"Good bye Tyrone, I am leaving. Tyrone, I will get home when I get home. I will see you later tonight." Vanessa is so mad at Tyrone that she slams the door.

"Are you crazy slamming the damn door like that?"

"I heard that Tyrone, I will slam the door anytime I feel like it. This is my house and there is nothing that you can do about it."

"That's what you think Vanessa." *What am I doing? I'm here yelling and she isn't even here. Now I have to laugh at myself. I need to speak to Kayla before I leave for the office. I think I will give her a shout out. Let me call her now.* "Hey Kayla, this is your lover man."

"Tyrone, how are you doing?   I miss you."

"I'm sorry about last night; the wife was standing nearby so I couldn't say what I wanted to say to you."

"I'm doing well, Tyrone. It's good to hear from you, are you on your way to work?"

"I should be, but I would like to see you before I go to the office. You make me feel so much better, especially after I have one of those heated arguments with my wife."

"So how long will it take you to get here?"

"If there is no traffic I should be there in about fifteen minutes."

"Okay I will be waiting for you." Kayla was already out the door and in her car, when Tyrone called. She couldn't wait to see him. "Wow that was fast! Woman get in here! I missed you so much."

"Yeah right, I bet you did, you didn't miss me that much otherwise you would have been with me last night and not with your wife."

"I wish I would have; a romantic night turned into a heated discussion and I'm really getting sick of it."

"What did your wife do to you now?"

"Well, last night she had the nerve to tell me that she wanted to go back to school and finish her degree. Now this morning she tells me that the firm wants her to work more hours, and she agreed to work more hours without running it by me first. How dare she!"

"So what's wrong with that? She should be allowed to go back to school and further her education. So what did you tell her?"

"I told her that I forbid it, and that she can't do it and that is what led to this mornings' spat."

"Truthfully Tyrone, I think you should let her do it."

"Wait a minute Kayla, whose side are you on anyway?"

"I'm on your side Tyrone; but just think about it, if your wife has more hours to work and she goes back to school that will give us more time to be together."

"You know I never thought about that, see that's why you are my woman."

"If you say so Tyrone."

"Kayla baby, I say so. Now come over here and give your man some of that good loving."

"This is the last time Tyrone. I'm not doing this anymore, it's been five years and yet nothing has changed. Either you leave your wife or I'm leaving you, and I truly mean it this time."

"How many times am I going to tell you, I just can't walk out on my wife; in due time, and don't threaten me like that again. I will leave her that I promise you."

"Yeah right, I'll believe it when I see it."

"Come here and let me make love to you. I want to put it in you and on you."

"Tyrone, did you hear that?"

"Did I hear what? Kayla honey, you are bugging."

"Tyrone, I could have sworn I heard the door to your house close."

"Baby you are hearing things."

"No I'm not Tyrone. I heard a door close."

"Kayla I don't hear anything."

"Tyrone, its Vanessa, are you here?"

Tyrone knows he has to be quiet, so he motions to Kayla to be quiet. One wrong move and all hell will break loose in the house.

"I see your car outside. Tyrone where are you?" *That's weird his car is in the driveway but he isn't here. I will call his cell. That's funny his phone is here, his car is here, but he is nowhere to be found. Hmm, something is not right, I can't pinpoint it but something isn't right. Let me check the kitchen. Okay he's not there. I forgot all about the basement, he is probably working out. He's not there okay. Where could he be? There has to be a logical reason. I have to go I am not going to think anything bad, maybe he just went for a morning run, or maybe he got a ride with one of the guys, but why would he leave his phone? Now I'm worried. I will call his phone again as soon as I get to the office.*

Vanessa realizes she forgot to set the alarm, but she can't turn back now. She has a meeting so she decides to set it from her phone; but she realizes that she can't set the alarm, it seems as though someone is in the house, but how can this be? Tyrone wasn't there a few moments ago. She has an uneasy feeling that something has gone terribly wrong, when she pulls up the surveillance system she realizes that the house is occupied she sees a strange woman in her house and she doesn't know who it is. Upon seeing this she calls the police and they immediately rush over to her house.

Realizing that time is of the essence, Tyrone tells Kayla that as much as he wants to make love to her he can't because he needs to get to work. As he puts on his tie, he realizes that someone is ringing his doorbell uncontrollably. Tyrone yells, "Who the hell is it?"

"Mr. Tyler it's Officer Scott, may I come in?"

Tyrone apologizes to Officer Scott for yelling. "Is everything alright Officer?"

"We received a call from your wife, stating that she saw a strange woman in the house when she pulled up the surveillance system. Is this true?"

"Yes Officer Scott, it is true. It's Ms. Kayla Jones, she is an attorney and she was just dropping off some papers for me to sign. I'm so sorry for the confusion."

"No problem, sorry for the mix-up, Mr. Tyler."

"Have a good day, Officer Scott."

"Take care and you have a good day as well Mr. Tyler, and you too, Ms. Jones."

"Whew Kayla, that was a close call."

"It sure was."

"Tyrone, you mean to tell me you have a

surveillance system that can be pulled up from your wife's job?"

"Yes, and I can pull it up from my job, sometimes we are in such a hurry and forget to set it from the house. We can set the alarm from our cell phones, laptops or our cars.

"That means she saw me in the house, that's a good thing."

"What do you mean it's a good thing? I don't want her finding out like this, it's better that I tell her in person; and I will do it just give me a little more time."

"Like I said Tyrone, I'm not going to take too much more of this. If you don't tell her then I will tell her."

"You better not mention a word of this to her. Do I make myself clear?"

"You know, she probably figured something was going on when she saw me inside the house. Well, I'm leaving anyway."

"I doubt it very seriously; and if Vanessa does mention anything to me about this, believe me I know what to tell her. Now come here and give me a kiss."

"Don't even think about it, good bye Mr. Tyler."

"What's with the Mr. Tyler?"

"You figure it out."

CHAPTER THREE

Vikki stops by Vanessa's office for a few moments. "Hey Vikki, let me tell you what happened.   I forgot to set the alarm for the house when I left this morning; and when I finally remembered it was around nine o'clock. I tried to set it from my phone, but it was showing up that the house was occupied, so I pulled up the surveillance system and I could have sworn I saw a woman in my house."

"So what did you do?"

"I called the police.   As a matter of fact, let me call them and find out what happened, then I will call Tyrone. I don't want to alarm him just yet. Hello, may I speak to Officer Scott, this is Vanessa Tyler.   I called you earlier about a suspicious woman in my house did someone from your precinct find out what was going on?"

"Yes Mrs. Tyler, I went over there personally and your husband was there. You were right, there was a woman there also. When I asked your husband about it he said that she was an attorney and that she had stopped by to drop off some papers for him to sign."

"Thank you so very much for all of your help Officer Scott. Have a wonderful day." Vanessa is puzzled by the phone conversation.

"Vanessa girl, what is wrong with you, what did Officer Scott say?"

"He said that Tyrone was at home, and Tyrone told him that the woman who was in my house was an attorney, who was dropping off some papers for him to sign."

"Yeah right, Vanessa. I believe that as far as I can spit, now you know what that means."

"No, I don't know what it means Vikki. Tyrone could be telling the truth; he has never given me a reason to suspect he is doing anything wrong."

"Vanessa if you don't think anything of it, and it's not bothering you, and you don't think anything is wrong then I won't bring it up again. Let's go out tonight, it will take your mind off of things."

"Nah girl, I can't. You go without me. I have some things I have to take care of."

"Yeah right Vanessa, like what? Look at you sitting there wondering if your husband is cheating on you. You said that Tyrone has never cheated on you; so get it out of your mind and let's go out. Let's have some fun, please."

"Okay Vikki, I guess you're right. I'm going against my better judgment. I'll go out with you, but you need to leave so I can finish my work. I'll see you about eight o'clock tonight."

"Okay girl, I will pick you up at your house, and Vanessa, it's going to be okay."

"If you say so; and Vikki, thanks for always being there when I need to vent. You are a good friend, I don't know what I would do without you. You give the true meaning of what a best friend really is."

Vanessa is on her way home from work. She wants to get there before Tyrone does she knows that if she doesn't it's going to be drama, and she doesn't want anything to spoil her much needed girls night out. Vanessa arrives in the nick of time; as soon as she kicks off her shoes Tyrone comes home. He gives his wife a long kiss, but she pulls away. Tyrone senses there is something wrong, but Vanessa lies and tells him that she had a long day at work. Vanessa heads upstairs to the bedroom; she is trying to pick out an outfit to wear tonight. But she is clearly distracted, she can't shake what Officer Scott had told her. Tyrone heads upstairs to the bedroom to talk to his wife, but before he can say anything she lets him know that she and Vikki are going out, and that Vikki will be at their house to pick her up soon.

Tyrone wants to know what is bothering her.

"Tyrone, there is nothing bothering me. I just have a lot going on at the job."

"Vanessa are you sure?"

She really doesn't want to say anything to Tyrone, but she manages to say it. "Actually there is something bothering me, but I don't want to make a big deal about it."

"Okay honey. I'm listening, so talk."

"I was on my way to work today, and I forgot some important papers, so I had to come back to the house to get them. Funny thing was when I got home, I saw your car in the driveway, and then I saw your cell phone on the table. It made me a little scared because I didn't see you at

all, and I checked the house. I left because I didn't want to be late for work; but for the life of me I could have sworn someone was in the house. I guess it was me being a worry wart so I just shook it off. But when I got to work I realized that I hadn't set the alarm for the house, and when I pulled up the surveillance system I saw a strange woman in the house."

"Why didn't you call me?"

"Tyrone how could I call you. I didn't know what was going on. Your cell phone was in the house on the table, I didn't know if something happened to you. I wasn't thinking clearly so I called the police, and asked them to come and check things out for me."

"Yes Vanessa, I know. I was still at home when they stopped by."

"Then why didn't you say something when I called out your name?"

"Vanessa darling, I was in the shower; now you know I can't hear anything in the shower."

"Honey you are so right, let me tell you what happened when I spoke to Officer Scott."

Strangely enough, he said that there was a woman in the house with you and that you told them that she was an attorney who happened to drop some papers off for you to sign."

It's true. Her name is Kayla Jones, she is an attorney, and I'm trying to get her company's business."

"Why did she come to our house… she couldn't catch you at the office? That doesn't seem right at all. I work for a law firm and all of the attorneys do business at the office, unless it's special circumstances."

"What are you insinuating, Vanessa?"

" Tyrone are you positively sure that she is just an attorney, and not more?"

"Vanessa, I don't like where this conversation is going and I'm going to stop it now. I said she is an attorney and I'm trying to get her company's business, that's all."

"Okay Tyrone, if you say so. I won't bring it up any more."

"And where do you think you are you going?"

"I told you that I'm going out with Vikki to have a little fun." Vanessa slips into a sexy black mini dress with four inch heels; she is looking fabulous with a body to die for. She is hoping that her husband doesn't notice what she has on, not that he would anyway. "Tyrone, she will be here in a minute. That's her I will call you when I'm on my way back home. Goodbye honey, I love you."

Tyrone now realizes what his wife has on. "Hold the hell up, you are not going out with Vikki or anyone else dressed like that go put on something else.   No wife of mine is going to be wearing clothes like that and I'm not there with her."

"Tyrone, in case you forgot, I'm grown and I can wear what I want to wear."

"Vanessa, either you put something else on or you won't leave this house tonight."

"Says who Tyrone?"

"Dammit woman, I said so! Now find something else to wear or you're staying home and that's final."

"Tyrone, I'm not changing my outfit. I look good in this and I am going to wear it and that's all there is to it."

"Vanessa, see if you leave this house tonight!"

"Oh Tyrone, I'm leaving… watch and see!"

"Vikki is outside waiting but I can tell her to leave. Now see if you get past me with that outfit on."

"Tyrone move."

"Move me!"

"Tyrone move out of my way now!"

"Vanessa, I said you are not leaving this house with that outfit on.

Now you can change and go out and have fun with your friend. Or you will just have to suffer the consequences if you keep that on."

"Tyrone, you get on my nerves."

"Vanessa baby, come here. I love you and you have many other outfits that fit you nicely. As a matter of fact, what about the red dress I got you last week?"

"Tyrone that dress is so plain and it doesn't show off anything!"

"That's the perfect dress. Hurry up, now I know you don't want to keep Vikki waiting. Vanessa you can get mad, roll your eyes, talk under your breath; but it is what it is. You are still my wife, and what I say goes."

Tears roll down Vanessa's face.

"Vanessa why are you crying? Don't look at it as a dictatorship look at it as a concerned husband. I have a reputation and it wouldn't look good if my wife is out on the town with her girlfriends, in something so revealing as that. What would people think, especially if I knew what you were wearing and I were not around? Hurry, you don't want to keep Vikki waiting; now wipe your face. Have fun, and Vanessa don't forget to check in with me. I love you and I'll see you when you get back."

Trying to keep the peace she tells Tyrone that she is sorry and that she doesn't hate him. "I do love you. See you later."

Vanessa and Vikki are out for a fun-filled time at Club Scene. Vanessa is sitting at a table when in walks a fine piece of dark chocolate. He approaches the table.

"Well hello, I'm Kevin, how are you?"

"Hello, I'm Vanessa, and I'm fine!"

"I know how you look; I asked how you were." Kevin is smiling.

"Kevin that was corny but cute, I'm great and you?"

"That's good to know that you are doing great, now what's a beautiful lady like you doing in a place like this?"

"I'm just here with my girlfriend Vikki, that's all; and before we go any further, I just want to let you know that I am a married woman. I'm not happily married, but I am married."

"Vanessa I'm sorry, but I must take this call. I will be back in a few moments."

Vikki says to Vanessa, "Girl you have got to cheer up, and who's your friend? He's cute, now I know you aren't stepping out on Tyrone."

"Girl, I'm just having a little fun conversation that's all it is."

" Kevin comes back over to finish his conversation.   Hello I'm sorry, but we didn't meet and you are?"

"My name is Vikki and it's nice to meet you."

"Vanessa I want to say that I am sorry that I had to walk away but, I had a very important call to take. Vanessa, I would really like to get to know you better. No strings attached, I'm just looking for a friend right now."

"Apology accepted, and I do understand that business does call," Vanessa says to Kevin, "that depends on what type of friend you are looking for."

"I'm just looking for someone I can talk with, that's all, is that a problem?"

"Kevin, I don't think it should be a problem, but let me think about it."

"Sounds fair. So Vanessa, let me guess. You're here because you have a feeling that your husband is cheating on you, and your friend dragged you here so you can get your mind off of your marriage for a little while."

"Actually, I'm not so sure that he is cheating, but my gut feeling is telling me that something is going on. He has never given me a reason to suspect that he is cheating on me, but I don't know what it is. My heart is telling me that I'm way off base, but my mind is saying something different."

"So let me ask you something, did you see him with another woman?"

"No I haven't actually seen him with another woman but there was a woman in my house today, and he claimed that she was an attorney who was dropping off papers for him to sign."

"Do you think that he maybe he is telling you the truth?"

"Maybe he is, maybe I'm just being a little paranoid."

Vikki says to Vanessa, "If you think he is doing something wrong then go with that, you know the old saying, 'if it quacks like a duck then it's a duck'."

"Kevin this is so strange that you know so much about what's going on in my marriage. Wait a minute, don't tell me you're a cheater, and now you're trying to have your cake and eat it too. Look here Kevin, if you don't get away from me, there is no telling what I might say."

"Hold up, I'm not married. My wife died in a car crash two years ago, and I'm just getting back into the dating scene. It has taken me a minute to get over her death. I miss her dearly. But I can't dwell on that too much. I have to move on, but she will forever be in my heart. I pray that God blesses me with a great woman."

Vanessa says to Kevin; "Oh okay, I'm sorry you were just about to catch a bad case. It's getting late, and I need to get home, otherwise my husband will start a fight if I'm not home at a decent time."

"He's cheating, stepping, creeping out on you or so you think, and you are going home like nothing is wrong."

"Look Kevin, I can't prove that he's done anything wrong. I have to believe what he says until I see it differently. Well, it was nice meeting you."

"Wait, Vanessa here's my number. Call me if you just want to talk or have lunch."

"I don't think I will need to talk, but I will keep your number, just in case."

"That's good enough for me, and I'll be waiting for that call."

Vanessa decides that she doesn't want to go home; she talks Vikki into staying out a little longer.

"Now Vanessa, you know Tyrone is going to kill you. I don't think we should be doing this."

"Vikki, first of all Tyrone will be asleep by the time I get home and after all the drama I had to go through with him tonight who cares what Tyrone will think. I want to have some fun and I'm going to have it. I will deal with Tyrone when I get home."

"Vanessa you better be absolutely sure. I love you, but you will not have Tyrone coming after me because you were out late."

"Vikki, I can handle my husband. Now let's live it up for a few more hours."

"Vanessa! Tyrone is going to lock you in the house for the next six months."

"Vikki you are too funny. Now let's party."

CHAPTER FOUR

Vanessa tries to sneak in the house quietly, so as not to wake up Tyrone, but with no avail.

"Woman where in the hell have you been, do you realize that it's one o'clock in the morning?"

"Tyrone, what is your issue? I'm home, calm your nerves and go back to sleep, I could have stayed out all night if I really wanted to."

"Vanessa, I wish you would have stayed out, woman don't play yourself."

"Tyrone, if you don't get out of my face coming at me all crazy like that when you claim that some attorney chick was just dropping papers off to you, yeah right… you're probably creeping with her."

"I told you before that I'm not sleeping around with anyone. When are going to get it through your head, that I love you?"

"Then act like it, or I'm done."

"You're done with what? Why are you so paranoid? Maybe you should see someone about that paranoia."

"You know you are right, and maybe you need to see someone also."

"What in the world are you saying woman?"

"Did I stutter? I'm saying that maybe we need to go to counseling to figure out where our marriage is going, and if we can save it before it's too late."

"Vanessa I'm not going to counseling, there is nothing to save in this marriage. Tyrone immediately changes the subject. You know what Vanessa, I got it! Maybe we just need to get away from everything and everyone for a few days, how does that sound? Just the two of us, no calls and no interruptions."

Vanessa reluctantly says, "I guess it sounds okay."

"What do you mean you guess it sounds okay? We need this, we are both stressed, we are arguing more than usual and I don't like it. Vanessa, you have been on edge lately and it's affecting your actions. You would never have come home this late."

"I'm on edge?" Tyrone you are the one who is on edge, I feel like I'm walking on egg shells. It's like you are taking me and this marriage for granted. You know what, come to think of it, let's get away. It won't hurt to get away for a few days. A getaway is what we both need to try and put our marriage back on track. But right now let's go upstairs, I'm tired and I have to get up in a few hours."

"Vanessa, we will talk about you coming in late. I'm just too tired right now. Let's go to bed. Love You."

"I love you too Tyrone. Good night." It's the next morning, and Tyrone seems to be in a loving mood.

"Good morning beautiful how are you doing today?"

Vanessa wonders what has gotten into him. "I woke up this morning, so I'm blessed." Vanessa is getting dressed, but she is thinking about Kevin.

Tyrone reminds Vanessa about the awards dinner. "Honey, please do not forget about tonight."

"Tyrone, what's going on tonight?"

"Vanessa how can you forget? You know tonight is important to me, it's that special awards dinner. *The Investment Banker of the Year Awards Ceremony* that you promised you would attend with me for the past two months."

"Honey, I am so sorry. I've had so much on my mind lately, that I forgot all about it; but I promise I will be there for you. I wouldn't miss this for the world. I've got to go work. I will see you tonight, love you."

"Woman, come here and give me some love." Tyrone holds Vanessa in his arms and says, "You know that you are the only woman for me.   I mean it. I love you." Tyrone slaps Vanessa on the butt as she walks out of the room.

Tyrone can't wait for Vanessa to leave, so he can call Kayla. "Kayla honey, I can't see you tonight. I have to go to an awards dinner with the wife, and you know that she is going to be a pain in my butt. I can't wait to see you, but you know we can't do anything until tomorrow. Bye my love."

"Tyrone, enough of this. I have got to go… goodbye. We can't keep going on like this, you have to tell your wife something."

"I will tell her when the time comes, but right now things are staying put."

"Okay, just so you know, things are going smooth with me and my friend."

Tyrone asks Kayla "What friend?"

"Tyrone I am grown and single and I don't have to ask you who I can see. Just know that I have someone who wants to have a real relationship with me, so stay in your miserable marriage."

"Girl, don't make me come over there in the middle of his conversation." Tyrone forgets what he's about to say.

Tyrone is so upset about what he's hearing that he tells Kayla, that he has to go. He slams the phone down, "Good-bye!"

Tyrone arrives at work but doesn't stay long in preparation for his awards dinner, he can't wait. And he is also thinking that what he is doing to Vanessa is wrong, but he can't seem to get Kayla out of his mind.

Vanessa is already home and getting dressed for the ceremony, she really doesn't want to go, but she doesn't want to let Tyrone down. She is tempted to call Kevin just to see how he's doing; she must admit that she had a good time talking with him last night.

Vanessa thinking out loud, "Which one of these dresses should I wear the red or the black? Hmm, decisions, I'm going with the red, because I'm red hot…………..ha ha!!!!!"

Tyrone enters the house and prepares to go upstairs. He doesn't expect his wife to be there, he is amazed. "Hey honey, what are you doing here?"

"Tyrone I live here, were you expecting someone else? Isn't tonight your awards dinner, I thought I would surprise you and get an early start.

Red or black?"

"Red of course. Red hot, like my red hot wife," Tyrone says with a smile.

"If you say so. I'm surprised that you are back so soon. I thought you would have come home like a mighty rushing wind, nerving me because you can't seem to get it together. I am actually proud of you."

"Honey let's go, I don't want to be late for my own awards dinner, it wouldn't look nice."

"Okay darling let's go." Vanessa's phone rings. "Let me see who this is." It's Kevin on the phone. Vanessa can't let on that it's a man on the phone so she has to play it cool and pretend that it's Vikki. She hopes that Kevin will be able to catch on. "Hey Vikki how are you?"

"Hello beautiful, it's Kevin. Is this a bad time for you to talk?"

"Yes it is. I'm on my way to an awards dinner for Tyrone can I get back to you later?"

"Sure you can baby, bye. I can't wait to hear from you. Okay, good night."

"Vanessa, who is that?"

"It's Vikki, checking to see what I'm doing; I told her that I would speak to her later."

The Tylers arrive at the awards dinner arm in arm, looking like a couple in love. You have to admit, they make a handsome couple. Tyrone is six feet tall and two hundred pounds of solid muscle. Vanessa is five feet three inches petite and a body that is the envy of every woman who sees her. Of course she turns heads wherever she goes, and tonight is no different. Tyrone leaves her alone for all of five minutes, and by the time he comes back to escort her to their table some stranger is hitting on her; and of course Tyrone is mad as hell!   He approaches Vanessa, and is about to scream at her, but he realizes that they are in public. He whispers in her ear that he will deal with her when they get home.

Vanessa is confused. She asks Tyrone, "What in the world are you ranting about?"

He tells her that he steps away for five minutes and some guy is in her face.

She asks him, "What am I supposed to do? Tyrone I can't help it that a man is attracted to me. Maybe if you felt that way about me, other men would sense it and wouldn't approach me. Tyrone, for the record I am not interested in any other man. So let's go to our table and enjoy a wonderful evening together. Can you at least do that for me?"

Tyrone still has an attitude. "What do you mean if I felt that way about you? What way do you think I feel about you?"

"Honey this is not the time, nor is it the place to discuss anything. This is your night and you are nominated for the most prestigious award of the evening, so let's enjoy. Thank you."

"Baby you are right."

Vanessa has her mind on other things and this dinner isn't one of them, she just wishes this night would be over sooner than later. The time is drawing near everyone is high with emotions on who will win the coveted Investment Banker of the Year Award. It is a tight race, but of course Tyrone wins the most prestigious award of the night. When he makes his acceptance speech he decides that he wants his wife to be by his side as he receives this award. She is shocked by the gesture but she willingly obliges.

Tyrone and Vanessa come home from the awards dinner; he helps Vanessa with her coat then he holds her in his arms. "Honey, I could not have won this award without you; you have been in my corner through it all and I love you for that."

"Well, what brought this on you never talk this passionate to me, are you cheating on me?"

"Woman, I told you before I am not cheating on you. I don't know why you would think I'm cheating."

Vanessa has this look like are you kidding me? "Because you want children and I can't give them to you, and that would make any man go astray."

"Well I'm not any man, and that doesn't matter to me." As Tyrone is saying this to his wife, he can't help but think about Kayla.

Hesitant! "Okay honey if you say so, then I believe you, you are a good man and by the way I am proud of you; you deserve this award you really worked hard for this!" Tyrone is tired, but he is in the mood for some loving; he works his way to the bedroom. "So Mrs. Tyler, I will meet you in the bedroom in five minutes."

"I'll be there in four minutes." Vanessa is all smiles.

"Don't keep me waiting."

"I won't, handsome."

Vanessa is all smiles after a romantic night with her husband. She is up with a smile on her face as she is getting ready to head to the office.

Vanessa decides she needs to talk, so she calls Vikki. "Girl I lied to Tyrone last night, I have never lied to him. I told him that I was on the phone with you, but it was Kevin who called me."

"Girl no you didn't, and what did you say to Kevin?"

"I basically told him that I was going to an awards dinner with my husband, and that I would speak with him later. Tyrone believed me when I said that it was you." Vanessa has a smirk on her face. "So what are we going to do tonight? We haven't gotten together in a couple of days. Meet me at my job at six o'clock. We can grab a bite to eat, and go to a club after that. I'm looking to enjoy myself and have some fun, and who knows who I might meet."

"But Vanessa, what about Kevin?"

"What about him? He is just a friend and that's all he is; remember I am still a married woman."

"Friend, yeah right! Vanessa you need to get know that brother and show him what you're working with. I'll talk to you later, see you in a couple of hours."

"Bye girl, see you soon." As soon as she hangs up the phone with Vikki, Vanessa's phone rings.

"Hey sexy, how is my girl doing?"

"I'm not your girl, but I'm okay."

"Excuse me, you're not my girl yet, but give it time."

Vanessa being sarcastic tells Kevin, "If you say so,

Kevin, is there something that you needed? I have to run an errand."

"I just wanted to see if we can get together tonight?"

"I'm actually having dinner with my friend from the other night, you remember her Vikki."

"Oh I do remember her, maybe I can meet you guys somewhere."

"I'll think about it, but I really must go. I will speak to you later. Good bye."

"Good bye for now."

"Okay don't hang up, wait a minute. You know what Kevin? That sounds like a good idea. I will call you later, and let you know where we are going. I really have to go, I promise to call you later. Goodbye now." Vanessa hangs up the phone and realizes that she has to get to her hair appointment at Desire's Hair Salon.

CHAPTER FIVE

As Vanessa is at Desire's she is waiting in the reception area to be called on. But of course, she doesn't wait very long. Delicious is the owner of Desire's Hair Salon. He immediately summons for Vanessa to come to the back. Sorry about that but I can't have my best customer sitting in the waiting room like that.

"Girl, where have you been? Bring yourself over here girlfriend, you need a touch up from the neck up."

"My hair isn't that bad, and it's only been a couple of weeks since you last saw me."

"More like a month, so tell me what's going on? So Vanessa, you still hanging in there with Tyrone. I would have left his trifling behind by now."

"Delicious now why would I leave my husband? I admit that I feel like he's hiding something from me. I have a strange feeling that more is going on than meets the eye with that attorney chick that was at my house; but he swears up and down that it is strictly business, so I have to take him at his word. I'm good."

"Okay what attorney chick? What happened Vanessa? The other day, I pulled up my surveillance on my phone and found a strange woman in my house. When I contacted the cops they went to my house, and Tyrone was there with this chick named Kayla Jones that he claims to be an attorney who was dropping off papers to the house. He said that nothing was going on between the two of them. I don't want to believe that he is cheating. I have to take Tyrone at his word."

"Chile like I said, you are good because I would have changed his name from Tyrone to No Nuts when I was finished with him."

"Delicious what in the world are you talking about?   Stop beating around the bush."

"Vanessa, word on the street is that your husband has a so-called trick. I mean a woman on the side, and he's been seen around town with her from time to time."

"Delicious, now you know how I feel about rumors. I don't like them and I don't believe it anyway so can we move on to a different subject."

Just as Vanessa says that, Kayla walks into the shop.   Delicious motions to her!

"Sista girl, I'll be with you soon, hold tight."

"Ok thanks." While Kayla is waiting, she gets a call it's Tyrone!

"Hi there, I'm at the hairdresser. I'm waiting to get dolled up for a certain man that I know."

"I'm already your man and baby you don't need to fix anything about you."

"I know that I don't need to fix anything about me, but I'm not getting dolled up for you. It's for a friend and he's not married. Look, now is not a good time to talk about this. I will speak with you later."

Tyrone hangs up the phone with a puzzled look on his face, he's not too pleased that Kayla is talking about another man. Tyrone knows that he has to put a stop to all this madness that Kayla is talking about.

Delicious says to Vanessa, "What are you doing tonight? You need to get your groove on."

"I'm going out with Vikki, seems like she has a new friend and I'm going to make sure things work out. I'm not getting my groove on with a man I don't know."

"Well Vanessa, if you get your groove on, then you will know him." Delicious is cracking up. "Oh I want to hear about Vikki's new man girl, give me the scoop." Vanessa begins to tell Delicious about Vikki's man, but decides against it.

"Delicious don't try to change the subject back to me getting my groove on, you ought to stop it. You know that I'm not that type of woman."

"Then you need to be a different type of woman."

"What in the world are you talking about?"

"Girl, I bet you are a freak in the bedroom, you are probably one of those Tri-Girls."

"Delicious I hate to ask 'but what is a Tri Girl'?"

"You'll try anything once and I say you need to try this guy you just might like it. Hmm, your husband is probably a try man."

"A Try Man'?"

"Yep he is trying to get his manhood on with his new trick."

"Delicious you are a mess, and you know that's not the case."

"Vanessa, you are so naïve you are getting on my last nerve acting like you don't know. I tell you he is doing something or someone else."

"Okay, enough is enough. Can we talk about something else? I'm getting upset I don't like where this is going!"

"Vanessa, I would never say anything intentionally to get you upset. You are my friend and I don't want you to be hurt. You are a good person and you deserve a good person in your life, that's all I'm saying."

"Delicious, I'm sorry for snapping at you. Thank you for those kind words. And girl this hairdo is fierce. Maybe my husband will want to make love tonight. I'm gonna put it on him. He won't know what hit him."

"Now that's how you do it Vanessa. You go girl and get yours tonight."

"Thanks again Delicious, for making me look great as always. I will call you later to make my next appointment. Kisses Delicious."

"Kisses two times to you Vanessa, now go home and rock your husband's world. Show him what you are working with," Delicious says, smiling.

Vanessa hops in her car; she looks too good to stay at home. She calls Vikki and tells her to meet her for dinner. She heads to Chez Vous one of her favorite spots. On her way there, she decides to contact Kevin. There is something about Kevin that just makes her day. "Hi Kevin, how are you?"

"Hey Vanessa, and to what do I owe the pleasure of this call?"

"Believe it or not I was thinking about you, and I wanted to see how you are doing."

"I'm good and I'm actually glad that you called. I missed speaking to you. I hope we can get together soon."

"That's sounds fine. I promise I will call you sooner than later."

"You do that."

"I will, and Kevin, it was nice speaking with you."

"Same to you, Vanessa."

"Damn, that man makes me hot just by the sound of his voice. Lucky for him I'm married."

Vanessa is so enthralled in thought about Kevin she almost forgets to call Tyrone to inform him that she is going to have dinner with Vikki. "Hi honey, it's me."

"Vanessa, I know who you are."

"I'm just calling to let you know that I'm going to dinner with Vikki."

"You have been spending a lot of time with Vikki."

"Tyrone she is my best friend. It's only for a couple of hours. I will be home by ten-thirty tonight."

"That must be some dinner, but we will discuss all this going out that you have been doing lately. It's fine this time go out and have some girl fun, okay baby enjoy."

"Thank you and I will."

Tyrone is happy about this, now he can see Kayla. He picks up the phone to dial Kayla. *Kayla, please pick up.* To his dismay, he has to leave a message on her voicemail. "Kayla where are you, I'm trying to call you? I want to see you tonight. Call me back as soon as you get this message." Tyrone can't wait for her to call back, so he decides to blow up her phone again. "Hey baby, where are you?"

Kayla finally answers his call, "Hey Tyrone, I got your message. I can't see you tonight. I told you I'm meeting a friend. I will talk to you later, and I do love you; maybe we can get together another time."

Tyrone slams the phone down. He can't believe Kayla is ditching him for another man; he is going to put a stop to this. *I know she isn't cheating on me with another man, well she has another thing coming.* He decides to call Kayla again.

"Tyrone what is it now is everything okay with you?"

"No Kayla, everything isn't okay. I miss you and I want you to come over here now. Cancel your date. I need to see you now. I want to make love to you. My wife went to dinner with her girlfriend; she won't be home until ten-thirty.   I'll make sure you are gone before she gets back."

"I don't know, that's playing it real close. I'm not so sure I want to come over, Tyrone. I have a great guy waiting for me."

"Cancel it and get over here tonight that's all that I'm going to say woman."

Tyrone is preparing for a romantic few hours alone with Kayla, the true love of his life.

Tyrone says out loud to himself "I can't wait for my baby to get here. I mean I love Vanessa but I'm in love with Kayla, and I eventually need to tell Vanessa the truth. I know it's wrong to have my cake and eat it too but what am I to do?   I am going to hurt the woman who has been with me for all these years, but she can't have my children."

The doorbell rings… it's Kayla.

"Hello babe, don't you look scrumptious. Well, are you going to stand there or are you going to get in here so I can wrap you in my arms?"

"Hey babe. It's good to see you.   I canceled my date for you so this better be good."

"What do you mean that you canceled a date for me? You are my girl so you shouldn't be seeing anyone else."

"If that ain't the pot calling the kettle black. You are still with your wife, and I'm your piece of tail. You think it's okay for you to do us both like this; yet I can't see anyone else. Tyrone you are tripping."

"I'm not tripping, I'm in love with you; and when the time is right I'm going to divorce my wife."

"Here we go again with the crap, well until you get it right I'm going to have friends so deal with it. Look, I'm sorry; but I am truly not feeling this right now. Maybe another time Tyrone, I really must go. You take care and I will call you in a day or two; but right now I'm going to see if I can reschedule the date with my friend that should have never canceled in the first place."

"Kayla I'm not happy about this other guy, but if you say he's just a friend then he better stay a friend; because if I find out that he is hitting on you, I am going to hit on him and not in a friendly way."

Deep down inside Kayla is in love with Tyrone, but she is kind of interested in Michael. Michael also happens to be her business partner, and she wants to see where this might lead.

"I said he's a friend, Tyrone."

"Let's keep it that way, Kayla."

Vanessa calls Tyrone. She knows that he is going to be livid when she tells him that she won't be home until later. Vanessa is hesitant to say anything to her husband.

"Hey darling, what's up?"

"Hmmm nothing."

"Yes it is Vanessa. I hope I'm going to like what you are about to say."

"Well you see, I know I told you that I would be home by ten-thirty, but that has changed. I want to go to Club Scene for a little bit with Vikki. Is that okay?"

"It's fine, we'll talk later."

She is shocked that he said yes. Vanessa wonders if this is going to cause an argument when she gets home.

Vanessa and Vikki are at Club Scene. Vikki says, "Vanessa isn't that your friend Kevin? I wonder what he's doing here."

"I invited him here; he's fun to be with and he is very good company."

"So you like this guy? There is nothing wrong in having a friend. If he makes you happy and you're not finding it from your husband, then I say 'do you boo'."

"I just don't feel right going behind Tyrone's back."

"Vanessa, girl let me put a bug in your ear, you know as well as I know that there is something a little fishy with that trick Kayla and your husband. Deep down inside, you know there is something going on so there is nothing wrong in having friends; or shall I say doing friends, because he's probably doing his friends. You are not doing anything wrong, so stop acting like you are doing something wrong."

"Yes I am doing something wrong, anytime you step out of your marriage it's cheating whether it's emotionally, physically or mentally."

"Vanessa you are hurting and you need to have some fun, so have a little fun; remember I got your back."

"Yeah, I guess you are right, Vikki. We are only hanging out and enjoying all these handsome men. And that Kevin… he is a friend, but girl he is fine, and look at that body…um um um um um."

Kevin says to Vanessa, "Hey beautiful it's good to see you, I'm glad you were able to get away from your husband."

Vikki says to Vanessa, "I'm going to leave and let you two be alone."

Vanessa says to Vikki, "Please stay, I don't know who might be watching me. You know Tyrone knows everyone, it's just better that way."

"Kevin, I hope you don't mind, I really don't like being the third wheel."

"Vikki I do understand, but there are exceptions to the rule and this is the exception."

Kevin asks Vanessa how her day went so far.

"It was hectic but there is no need to complain. Can you believe that I work four to five hours a day, and it seems like I work a full time job?"

"So what do you do?"

"I am an Executive Assistant I work for a small, but thriving law firm; it gives me something to do. It beats staying home all day."

"Girl you have it made you have a husband who is successful and three nice homes and cars, and whatever you want."

"Yeah, but I don't have kids and that's what is missing; and I have a husband who acts like he's afraid to touch me. He acts like I am less of a woman because I can't have kids."

"Well you will never have to worry about me cheating, because I believe in making a woman happy in all areas of her life, it's about her. My goal is to please the woman I'm with, if she's happy, then I'm okay."

"Do you have any brothers?"

Vanessa tells Kevin that he better stop talking like that otherwise, we might have to get serious. Vanessa is laughing to herself as she is saying this.

"Vanessa anytime, anyplace and anywhere, you ain't said nothing but a word. I'm here for you and when you get tired of being treated badly by your husband you know where I am, you have access to my email, Facebook, Twitter, Instagram, cell, car phone, home number; don't hesitate to use any and all of them if you have too."

Vanessa looks at her watch and realizes she needs to get home as soon as possible.

"Vikki, girl I have to get out of here I told Tyrone that I would be home by ten-thirty and I don't have time to argue with him tonight ."

"Okay girl, let's go but before we do, there is a cutie who has been staring at me all night long. I'm going to give him the digits."

"Okay, Vikki but make it fast. You are a mess."

Kevin says out loud, "Wow! Who does that?"

"Vikki is a true friend, and she is single, and she has a great job, and of course she has a slamming body; she can get any guy she wants, she has been hurt so much. So right now she is just going to date. I can't wait until she finds someone so she can find some happiness in her life."

"Girl, now we can leave. I have his number, and he has mine, but you know I don't call a man, never that, he has to do the pursuing…"

"What about your new friend? What's his name Antonio?"

"We are friends right now, so until things change in the relationship, I'm still available."

"Check please, well ladies I had a good time with the both of you, and Vanessa I truly look forward to seeing you real soon, maybe tomorrow. Whenever you can slip away, but don't let it be too long."

"Vanessa, now he's a keeper."

"Yeah I know he is; but I'm married and that changes the nature of the game. Vikki, I'm in no mood to argue with Tyrone tonight." As the ladies are about to leave the club, Kevin doubles back to the surprise of both ladies. They both want to know what happened. Kevin says "Where are my manners?" I can't leave and not make sure that you ladies make it to your cars safely, so I am going to drive the both of you ladies to you cars and make sure you get in them okay. And I want to make sure you get home safe. Is that okay?" Both of the ladies are in agreement with Kevin.

Vanessa knows this guy is a dime a dozen. Her mind is telling her to leave him alone, but her heart is telling her to take a chance on love. Vanessa realizes that although she is unhappy in her marriage, she took vows and she can't and won't step out of her marriage for anything or anyone.

Kayla decided to stop by and see Tyrone after her dinner date with Michael. She knows that she shouldn't be there. It won't be for long anyway.

"Hey Kayla, what are you doing here?"

"Well my dinner date ended early and I thought I would stop by for a very brief night cap."

"Well we still have about another hour. So let's make the most of it. I am so glad that you came over here. I really miss you."

"I miss you too."

Tyrone and Kayla get comfy and cozy on the bed.   In the middle of them wanting to make love, Tyrone's phone rings. It's Vanessa. "Damn babe, let me take this. Hey Vanessa is there something wrong?"

"No nothing's wrong, I just decided to come home early I will be there in about fifteen minutes." Tyrone realizes that Kayla is going to be heated when he tells her this. He chooses not to, hoping to get in at least five minutes of some type of pleasure.

Kayla calls for Tyrone to come and sit next to her, she is giving him a massage and it's feeling good. He opens his eyes and realizes that Kayla has to leave. "Hey baby, Van just called me and she will be home in about fifteen minutes. I love you babe and I promise this is going to work out."

"Since when did you start calling your wife Van?"

"That's been my nick name for her since we've been married, is there a problem with me calling my wife Van?"

"Men usually have nick names for their wives when they actually are in love with them, not when they are cheating on them."

"Look I'm tired of doing this sneaks and peeks. You need to make up your mind, because I might not be around anymore."

"Like you're leaving me for someone else. Woman, I told you before I don't have time for your nonsense. I'm going to take care of it; now please get dressed before my wife, I mean Van, catches you."

"Don't you mean before she catches us."

"Whatever!   Just leave sweetie."

Kayla is getting dressed and making her way out of the house; she barely gets out before Vanessa arrives.

"Hello Tyrone, are you here baby?"

"I'm upstairs in the bedroom."

"I will be right there."

Tyrone is clearly lying to his wife. "Woman, what took you so long to get home? I was waiting for you."

Vanessa is distracted by what Tyrone is saying. "Something seems different about the room and I can't pinpoint it."

"It does? Well something is different. I changed the sheets and I moved the chair from one side of the room to the other."

"No, that's not it; but the room does look nice."

"Honey let's just go to sleep, I'm tired."

Vanessa says okay, but she is puzzled; she is feeling a little bit uncomfortable. "Maybe it's just my imagination."

"Honey what did you say?"

"Nothing, I'm just thinking out loud, you know that I talk out loud randomly."

"Yeah, I know, good night baby girl."

"Good night honey."

Vanessa is still puzzled about the night before. She decides that she wants to go in to work early. She has to call Vikki as soon as she can, she needs to talk her. Vanessa gives Tyrone a kiss on the cheek. She rushes out the door as quickly as she can. "Goodbye Tyrone. I have to go. I didn't realize how late it is, I have a very important meeting that I have to get to. Talk to you later."

"Take care sweetie have a good day." Tyrone immediately calls Kayla.

"Is this the woman of my dreams? I miss you and I can't wait to see you again."

Vanessa doubles back, she forgot something, "Tyrone who are you on the phone with?"

Tyrone says, "I'm on a business call, you know those business calls!"

"Okay, but I don't understand why they can't wait until you come in to the office to discuss business with you."

"Vanessa you know that's the world we live in."

"So true, this time I'm out for good. I will see you tonight."

"Bye, love you." Tyrone gets ready for work. Tyrone arrives at work for a business meeting, but when he arrives at the office he is informed that his scheduled meeting has been canceled.

Tyrone is irate! "I want to know who canceled this meeting. And why wasn't I informed." In the middle of his tantrum he receives a phone call.

It's Kayla on the other line.

"Good morning darling, how are you doing?"

"Kayla this isn't a good time, I had a very important business meeting, and it was canceled."

"Calm down I know all about your business meeting. I was the one who called the meeting, and I was the one the who canceled the meeting. Actually the meeting isn't canceled I just moved it to a more quiet location, and I'm sure that you don't mind."

"That's why I'm in love with you girl, you know what I need and when I need it. I will see you in about 30 minutes. Be ready for some good loving."

"If you say so, Tyrone you are the one who needs to be ready."

"Woman when it comes to you, I am always ready."

"Okay we need to get off the phone so that I can get there and try to make the most of the time that we will have together."

"Try to make the most of the time. I think you mean that we will make the most of our time together. I'm leaving work now."

Meanwhile Vanessa is on the phone with Vikki. "I didn't want to say anything but remember the other night when we went to the club? I left to go home and when I got there I went upstairs in the bedroom and Tyrone was there but it seem liked something was out of place in my bedroom, like someone had been there, and moved or took something from the room. When I mentioned it, Tyrone said that he put on some new sheets and that he moved the chair from one side of the room to the other side of the room. I agreed with it but I didn't believe it at all."

"Girl you have been stressed out lately, let me ask you something. Were a different set of sheets on the bed? And was the chair on a different side of the room?"

"Yes it was, and it made the room look so much better." Vanessa giggles.

"There you go see you have nothing to worry about, on to another subject are we going out tonight?"

"I'm not sure, I think I just want to relax at home."

"Girl come on, I have someone I want you to meet. His name is Antonio and we have been talking for a few months. I like him, and I want my best friend to meet my new guy."

"So, I guess this means that the status of your relationship has been upgraded, and you are no longer available."

"Well I think so. I'm still taking it slow, but he could be the one. I feel totally different when I'm with him. Please come and meet him, I'm sure that you will like him."

"You pulled my leg. I should call Kevin, he always seems to put a smile on my face these days. You know what girl, you are on. Let me tell Tyrone."

Vanessa is trying to get in touch with her husband, but he is not answering, and this is bothering Vanessa because Tyrone usually answers her on the first ring.

Tyrone's phone goes into voicemail. "Tyrone this is your wife, I'm trying to call you, but once again you're not answering. Well I just want to let you know that I'm going out with Vikki for a couple of hours. She has a friend she wants to introduce me to; and yes, Vikki is interested in someone, finally."

"Kayla girl, come here and let me look at you, I don't know why you even have that on. I'm going to tear it off in a few moments."

"Tyrone you know exactly what to say. So was that clever of me to schedule a business meeting with a fake new client? Damn, I'm good."

"You are so right about that, now woman come here." His phone is vibrating on the table. "Who in the world could this be?"

"Tyrone please don't answer it."

"Kayla, at least let me see who it is, it could be the office." When he picks up the phone he realizes that it's Vanessa, and she has been blowing up his phone. Vanessa baby is something wrong, are you okay?"

"Yes, I'm okay. I've been trying to call you, and you didn't answer the phone I thought that was kind of strange."

"Yeah, I got your voice-mail."

"Now you know when I'm in a big closing I don't answer the phone. I have to get back to my client did you need something?"

"Nothing important, I just wanted you to know that I'm going out with Vikki. She has a friend she wants me to meet."

"It's about time that she is dating someone; he might be the man to change her outlook on relationships. Maybe she will start trusting again. And not be around us so much."

"Yes, maybe you are right. I hope and pray that he isn't playing with her feelings."

"Let me know how this guy is."

"I'll let you go, bye, see you later."

"Bye baby."

Kayla is angry about the fact that Tyrone just said bye baby to his wife. "You know what! I'm going to leave, I can't stomach the lies anymore. I'm not going to keep sharing you like this!"

"Babe I'm all yours, so you have nothing to worry about at all."

"Did you forget you have a wife, and until you divorce her, I'm not all yours. You know what? This is it, you need to make up your mind. Look here, you have two months to tell your wife what's going on, or I will tell her."

"You wouldn't dare."

"Tyrone, try me!   I'm tired of this little trivial game that is being played by you. You're a grown man playing a kids game. You have two months to get it right, or we are through and I mean that!"

"Don't threaten me!"

"It's not a threat, it's a promise. Look I'm ready to go, I'm not feeling this anymore, plus I have to meet someone here in a few minutes."

Tyrone is upset at the situation. "Yeah I better get back to the office." He knows that he has to do something otherwise Kayla is going to walk out of his life for good.

Tyrone and Kayla leave the hotel. Delicious happens to be there for a hair convention. He knows who Tyrone is, but Kayla he's not feeling.

Delicious is being sarcastic. "Well hello Mr. Tyler, how are you today?"

"Hello Lavell, how are you? Fancy meeting you here today!"

"The name is Delicious. I am great and I'm here for the hair show and what are we here for today?" He is being nosy.

"I'm here for a business meeting."

"I bet you are Tyrone."

Tyrone introduces Kayla to Delicious. "Excuse me; anyway this is Kayla Jones, and we were just wrapping up a meeting."

Delicious mumbles under his breath, "I bet you were wrapping up something, but it wasn't a meeting". He thinks there is more to this than meets the eye, and he is about to speak on it when Michael walks up.

Kayla introduces Michael to everyone. "Tyrone Tyler, this is my business partner Michael Thomas and Michael, this is Tyrone. He's trying to convince me to let his firm handle our company's business."

"Maybe he can convince you Kayla."

"She is hard to convince."

"You're right Michael; that she is. She is one tough cookie… so do I have the account or not?"

"As far as I am concerned, you have it; but Michael has to agree to it also."

"Mr. Tyler, it's a done deal."

"You guys won't regret it."

Michael says to Tyrone "Oh I know we won't regret it; and by the way, whatever you need, you can have it."

Tyrone says, "I like the way that sounds."

"Kayla, I know you dropped off papers for me to sign a while ago, I will get them officially signed today."

"Thanks man, I will stop by your office and pick them up."

"You do that, Michael."

"It was nice meeting you Tyrone."

"Same here brother, maybe we can go out for a congratulatory drink."

"That sounds great, Michael."

"Sorry, but I have to get home or my wife will start to wonder where I'm at." Tyrone doesn't realize that Michael is the friend that Kayla has been dealing with for the past two months.

"I'm sorry Michael, where are my manners? This is Delicious."

"It's nice to meet you and Kayla, especially you Mr. Thomas. I like that name *Tom mas* and yes, I must get to know Mr. Thomas," Delicious says smiling.

Delicious says to Tyrone before he leaves, "Please forgive me for what I was thinking about you and Ms. Jones."

"Delicious, I will let it go this time; we have all jumped to the wrong conclusions from time to time, so no worries at all."

"Tyrone will you please tell your wife to call me; she had an appointment with me, but she missed it."

"I definitely will, that's weird; that's not like Vanessa to miss her hair appointment. I'll get to the bottom of it. Thanks and ttyl my brother."

"MMMMM, that sounds scrumptious."

"Lavell, it means ttyl (talk-to-you-later). Get your mind out of the gutter.'

"Don't worry, that's not where my mind is."

"Well, I really have to get going. Once again it was nice meeting you Michael, and thanks again Kayla."

"You are welcome."

Delicious says out loud, "Who does he think he's talking to? I'll believe that as far as I can spit. Yeah right, business partner my foot…Michael and Kayla may be the business partners, but Tyrone you and Kayla have a lot more going on. I'm going to get down to the bottom of this."

Michael says to Kayla, "Girl you look so good, let's get out of here I'm hungry."

"Okay, but I'm not really hungry, maybe we can run across the street and get something to drink." Kayla and Michael exit The Rendezvous Hotel to head to the coffee shop.

Delicious has decided to head over to the coffee shop with one of his friends Shaniqua. "I just saw my friend's husband with another woman, but they claim that they were only having a business meeting."

"Well Delicious, maybe they were having a business meeting."

"I think there was more to it than that, but I can't say for sure that it is."

"I did meet the business partner, so maybe there isn't anything going on, but something doesn't seem right."

"Girl cool it, if you saw the business partner, then maybe there was a meeting going on."

"Yeah you're right, but you know when my radar detects something, it's usually right. Let's just order something." As soon as they say that Vanessa and Vikki walk in.

"Well, well, well, look what the cat dragged in. Vanessa where in the world have you been missy, you missed my appointment?"

"I have been so busy with work and you know you are right, I totally forgot, I am so sorry. Please forgive me."

"I will excuse you this time, but never again. Well this must be my lucky day, two Tylers in one day."

"Delicious, what are you talking about?"

"I just ran into your husband, he said that he was coming from a business meeting."

"Well then, where is he?"

"He just left, that must have been some meeting."

"What are you talking about Delicious? You always stretch things."

"Well when I first saw him, it was him and this nicely dressed tramp, I mean woman. She was playing Tyrone close, they seemed lovey dove with each other. I startled Tyrone. I could tell he was up to something because he called me Lavell."

Vanessa says to him, "Isn't that your name?"

"Yes it is, but the only other time your husband ever called me Lavell was when he was trying to keep a secret from you."

"What secret has he been keeping from me?"

"It's a secret that I'm not supposed to tell. Anyway, that's not important, that was over ten years ago. I was trying to question him, but before I could say something this deep dark chocolate hunk of a man came over and I'm introduced to Ms. Jones so-called business partner."

"Delicious, what is the guy's name?"

"I believe his name is Michael Thomas, and I must get a hold of that; that just makes me shake all over. He can handle my business any day."

"Tyrone is trying to close a business deal, with some company called TJ Associates and Kayla Jones is the attorney who is handling the contracts and she does have a business partner. I believe that his name is Mr. Thomas, but I'm not sure, so it probably was nothing".

"Yeah, it probably wasn't anything, but you never know.   Ladies who is this HUNK OF MAN that is coming this way?"

Vikki tells Delicious that it's her friend and his name is Antonio.

"Well he can tone me up anytime," laughing out loud.

"Fool sit down and be quiet, he's straight."

"And I know how to make him crooked."

"You are not well. Vikki is smiling."

"Hello ladies."

"Hello."

"And you are?"

"Checking out the goods, I mean for my friend. Girl…Vikki, he passed my inspection in more ways than one."

"Vikki, what in the world is he talking about? It's good to see you."

Delicious is looking at Antonio in a seductive manner. "I bet it is."

"I do believe that I was talking to Vikki."

"My bad. I really have to go, because if I don't I'm going to start imagining things about Antonio that I shouldn't. Bye y'all, and a special good-bye to you Antonio."

Antonio says to Vikki that Delicious is creepy, "Let's get out of here."

Vanessa says, "Yes, let me get home. I know that Tyrone is there having a fit because I'm not there to greet him."

Delicious says sarcastically "Greet him? Is he a King or something?"

"Delicious, sometimes he thinks so; but I have been married so long that I know how to handle him, when he starts fussing."

Vikki says, "Girl you are not his maid. You are his wife."

"Vikki, I think he knows that already."

Vikki tells Vanessa the following, "that's not a marriage; it sounds more like a controlling dictatorship."

"Look I have ten minutes to make it home. I have to drive like a speed demon. Please pray for me. Love you both, nice meeting you Antonio."

"Same to you Vanessa, now get home safe.

Vanessa please don't forget to call me to let me know that you made it home okay."

"I promise I will call you when I'm home."

CHAPTER SIX

"Vanessa where have you been, I was worried about you?"

"Tyrone I called you."

"Woman don't lie to me, you didn't call me."

"Tyrone are you losing it? I called you and when you didn't answer I left a message on your voice-mail, and I called you again, and you finally picked up the phone. Did you forget that you spoke to me."

"Tyrone is hesitant to say anything. You know baby you're right. I have so much going on that I forgot that we spoke to each other, but you didn't call me after that.

I would have, but you said you were in an important meeting and I didn't want to bother you again. Plus it wasn't that important; I just wanted to let you know that I met Vikki's new friend. You totally didn't remember that conversation at all."

"By the way, how is the guy?"

"I think she finally met someone that she really likes, and he is really into her. I hope she doesn't mess this up."

"Me too, she sure can mess up a relationship."

"Tyrone, now that's not nice to say about my friend, even though it's true. By the way, I ran into Delicious today."

"You did, and how is he doing?"

"Tyrone, you don't know?"

"What do you mean by that?"

"Delicious said that he ran into you and that attorney Kayla Jones today, and he said you introduced the two of them and that he also met her business partner; but Delicious seems to think that there was more to it than that."

"Delicious likes to exaggerate things, nothing is going on with me and Kayla."

"Who said that there was something going with you and that Kayla woman? Wow, you are really being defensive.   You'd think that you and she were having an affair. He said that he thinks there is something more than her and this Michael being just business partners."

"Oh so he thinks that they are more than business partners… he doesn't seem like her type."

"How do you know what her type is?"

"Because I saw her today, and she was all over this other guy, she said that she likes her men tall."

"You'd never know you weren't my type and look how long we've been married.   I was drawn to your heart."

Vanessa changes the subject. "So did you get it?"

"Get it, get what? Honey what are you talking about?"

"Did you get the account?"

"I told you earlier that Kayla and Michael are my new clients."

"That's my man! I'm glad that you got the account because you're great at what you do. Let's go to sleep. It's been a really long day."

"That's the best thing you have said all day. I'm so tired, I don't want to eat."

"Tyrone Tyler not hungry? Now I know you are tired."

"Ha ha Vanessa, you got jokes. I will let you have that one." Tyrone is thinking about Kayla while he is talking to his wife. He knows that he has to end this marriage, but he just can't bring himself to tell Vanessa that he isn't in love with her anymore, and that he hasn't been in love with her for a long time now. Tyrone gets out of bed and goes downstairs to clear his mind, but as usual he decides that he needs to talk to Kayla. Tyrone is playing it close by calling her on the phone while his wife is upstairs in the house sleeping; she could wake up at any time.

Meanwhile Kayla and Michael are together at Kayla's place.

"Michael honey, thanks for picking up the contracts for me. It was good that you got the chance to meet Tyrone."

"Kayla dear, I don't like him."

"Michael how can you say, that? You don't know him. Look, I was able to get his business, and that's all that matters."

"Maybe you were trying to get business, but it was a little more for him. I saw the way he was looking at you."

"Michael will you please stop tripping. Don't you know that you are the only man for me?"

Kayla loves Michael, but she is in love with Tyrone. She seems distracted.

"And let's keep it that way. Because if I find out that you and him are messing around it won't be good for either of you, especially not for him."

"Michael you are the one that I'm with totally." Kayla's phone rings, it's Tyrone.

"Hello oh hi, I can't talk right now, I will call you back." Kayla slams the phone in Tyrone's ear.

Tyrone is puzzled by Kayla's actions. He calls her again, because he wants to get the bottom of this.

"Hey darling it's me, you hung up the phone on me."

"I said I can't talk right now; I will speak with you later." Kayla slams the phone in Tyrone's ear again.

Michael says to Kayla, "Honey is everything okay?"

"Yeah, some guy is harassing me, but I'm going to be okay."

"Do you want me to call the cops?"

"No that's alright; I will let you know if I need assistance. Thanks, I love you so much."

"And Kayla you know that I love you, for the first time, I think I have found my true soul mate." Michael pulls Kayla close to him and kisses her.

"Michael, what was that for?"

"That was for us. I've got to get to the office, I have some business to take care of. I'll see you when you get there."

"Michael honey, do you have to go to the office? I thought that we could… you know." (Kayla has a big smile).

"I know what, Kayla? Are you trying to be fresh?" "Yes, I'm trying to be fresh. So how about a little love making?"

"Girl, you are making me hot."

"That's exactly what I want to do."

Michael begins to caress Kayla. He slowly kisses her, slowly working his way down her body.

"Oh Michael, that's my spot. Don't stop." Kayla screams out in pleasure. "Yes Michael!"

Michael asks Kayla, "Baby do you like it?"

"Yes I do Michael."

Michael's phone rings. He didn't realize it but he is late for his appointment. *Damn who can this be?*

"Mr. Thomas we have a one-thirty appointment."

"Mr. Lyle, I am so sorry. I will be there in twenty minutes. I'm stuck in traffic. Damn, Damn Damn! Baby I'm sorry about this you know that I love you. I will see you when you get to the office." Michael gives Kayla a kiss on the forehead.

"Okay baby, I love you too. I'm going to relax for an hour, then I'll be in, I have a client that's coming to the office, I will need you to sit in on the meeting."

"Sure thing baby, see you at the office." Michael leaves for his meeting.

No sooner than Michael leaves, Tyrone is at the front door.

Tyrone is seething because he wants to know why Kayla hung up the phone on him. He rings the bell, like he's lost his mind. Tyrone yells "Kayla open the door!"

"Tyrone what the hell is wrong with you?"

"Kayla I want to know why you nearly chewed my head off when I called you today. What in the hell is going on?"

"Tyrone how dare you take that tone with me. Michael and I were busy going over some documents for a very important meeting, and you kept interrupting us."

"Why didn't you say so! All you said was I can't talk. You didn't say that you were in a meeting. I would have waited to speak to you later."

"Tyrone I did, but you acted like you didn't understand what I was saying."

"Did something happen between you and Michael?   Because I have never seen you act like this before."

Kayla is lying; she tells Tyrone that nothing happened between her and Michael.   "I just have this big project that I have to finish for a new client, and I'm stressed."

"Well come give your man some good ole loving."

Kayla reluctantly gives Tyrone a kiss.

"Kayla something is wrong and I can't exactly pinpoint it, and I'm sure it has something to do with Michael."   Tyrone gives Kayla this strange look, "Michael is more than your business partner, Michael is attracted to you."

"Umm, I can't help it if a man is attracted to me."

"You are right and you can't help it that you are sexy as all heck; and truth be told, I don't mind that he is attracted to you, but for some reason I still think it's more to it than that. Kayla are you sure you and him were discussing business only and there was no pleasure?"

"I can't believe you would say that, you know what Tyrone, please just leave."

"I'm sorry babe, I didn't mean that, it's just that I get upset when I think of you with any other man but me."

Kayla says to Tyrone, "You are joking me. You're with your wife whom you can't stand to be with, and you are upset because another man is interested in me. If that ain't the pot calling the kettle black… what a joke."

"You know what Tyrone, please leave my house. I'm not trying to deal with you right now, I have to get ready to go to the office. I have a crucial meeting to attend, and I don't want to be late. I will speak to you later on."

"Kayla babe I am sorry, I didn't mean to aggravate you. Tyrone it's okay, now leave."   In the meantime Vanessa is running late for her hair appointment; she is in need of a makeover.

Vanessa stops by Desire's Hair Salon. "Hello Delicious, I'm here for my appointment."

"Come and have a seat and, how are you today girl, and how is that husband of yours?"

"He's okay, just a little busy with his new clients."

Delicious says under his breath, "I bet he is a little busy with his new client."

"Girl, what did you say?" Kevin unexpectantly comes to the salon.

"Hello, I'm looking for Vanessa Tyler." The Receptionist points to the back of the salon.

"Here comes that hunk of milk chocolate. I knew you couldn't resist."

"Sorry, but I'm not here to see you, I'm here to see Mrs. Tyler."

"Ooooooooooooh. Vanessa are you creeping on your husband?"

"No, I'm not creeping on my husband. Kevin is just a friend of mine. What are you doing here?"

"You left your wallet in the coffee shop last night and I wanted to return it, or did you rather I return it to your house?"

"Please no. Thank you so much for holding on to it I'm so glad that you came here instead."

Kevin is curious and asks, "Delicious why is your shop called Desire?"

"Because one taste of me and you will desire some more of this deliciousness."

Everyone cracks up laughing.

"Okay now, well that's my cue."

"Milk Chocolate don't leave, please stay I promise not to bother you."

"That's okay I have to get back to work. Vanessa maybe we can get together tonight."

"I'm not sure that's going to be a good idea, but I will call you, if I can get out. Once again thank you for returning my wallet, and we will talk soon."

"Until we speak later, Vanessa. It was nice seeing you, Delicious."

"No the pleasure is definitely all mine."

"Well, well, well, seems like someone has an admirer. Vanessa go for yours. What are you waiting for, give him some, and some more and some more."

"Delicious, you are completely out-of-control. I'm married."

"And so is your husband, and like I said before I think he's creeping. I bet you that he's getting some."

Shaniqua, an employee at Desire's, asks Vanessa if she wants to know if he's creeping.

Vanessa says emphatically. "Yes, please school a sista."

"Well, if he is always peeping out where you are going, what time you are coming back, and who you are with then he's creeping. He's trying to find out how long he has to get his groove on; watch what I tell you."

"Girl, I know you love your husband, but he is a man, a very fine man, but a man."

"What are you thinking about Tyrone? Oh, I'm not thinking about him cheating, I'm thinking about something totally different."

"I know he's straight, but a girl can dream."

"Delicious, he's straight as a nail."

"And a nail can be bent if it's hit in the right spot."

"Delicious you are no good, but you always make me look fabulous."

"I'm glad I could help, now go and give Mr. Brown some of that sweet stuff."

"As much as I would like to, I'm still married. I took vows and I'm going to honor them, through thick and thin. I'm going home to my husband."

"Vanessa, since I can't convince you to spend some time with Mr. Brown, I'm going to leave that alone. But I know you want to get revived and I don't mean with Vivarin." – laughing.

"Delicious, if my situation was different I would surely give Kevin anything that he wanted. Anyway, thank you for my fabulous hair do. Let me call and check on Vikki."

The phone is ringing. Vikki finally picks it up she is out-of-breath.

"Hello Vikki, how are you?"

"Hey girl it's me, did I interrupt something?"

"No Vanessa, I'm good."

"Are you sure?"

"Yes, I'm sure I just finished working out, how are you doing?"

"I'm alright. I just wanted to see if you wanted to go out tonight?"

"I can't, I have a date."

"Vikki, you have a date with whom?"

"Remember my friend Antonio? I really like him so I am going to spend some time with him."

"Well, you behave yourself."

"Do I have to?"

"No you don't, but do it anyway."

"Vanessa, I'm going to bring him by the house tonight."

"Not a problem I will see you both later. I've got to get home. You know how Tyrone is. He doesn't notice my new hairdo, but he will notice if dinner isn't on the table. He better be glad that I'm a faithful wife because I might be out there doing things and not with him. I was almost tempted to do something with Kevin."

"Why didn't you, Vanessa?"

"The thought of hurting Tyrone crossed my mind."

"Do you really think that he's considering your feelings? He's not at all."

"I can't be like him. Listen I am home now, we have to finish this conversation a little later on tonight."

"Tyrone is in a good mood for some reason, or so he's acting like it. He has even attempted to cook dinner."

"Honey something smells good in here, what is all of this?"

"This is for my lovely wife whom I wanted to do something special for; is that okay?"

"Sure it's okay, now tell me what's wrong."

"Why must something be wrong?"

"Because you don't cook for me like this and you haven't been this romantic in such a long time."

"Vanessa nothing is wrong. Can a man do something good for his wife?"

"Yes, you can do something good for me any time you want, and I love this new you deep down inside." However, she can't seem to shake what Delicious said earlier.

"And your hair looks wonderful."

"You're complimenting my hair? Vanessa says with a smile. Now I know something is wrong".

"Will you stop it and enjoy the evening; it might not happen again." Tyrone laughs-out-loud.

"You are so right about that, I'm going to bask in this for a long time;

and honey, I just want to say thank you for making this such a wonderful night thus far."

"Vanessa, you are so very welcome. Now let's go upstairs and enjoy the rest of the evening." Just as they are about to go upstairs Tyrone's phone rings. "Who in the world can this be?"

"Tyrone Tyler here, how may I help you?   That will have to wait, no I can't. I'm with my wife tonight, I'm sorry I will see you tomorrow morning at the office."

"Honey who was that?"

Tyrone tells his wife it was one of the guys at the office. But it was actually Kayla. She is talking sweet nothings over the phone. She is driving Tyrone wild, he quickly hangs up because he is getting turned on and he doesn't want to make an excuse and leave Vanessa alone for the rest of the evening.

"Why are they calling this late at night?"

"Baby who knows but I got rid of them. Tonight is your night, and I want you to enjoy it, without any interruptions. Is that okay?"

"Honey, that's fine by me, no more interruptions. Now let's get it on."

"Vanessa, look at you being frisky."

"Yep that's me, Vanessa "Frisky" Tyler, ha ha ha."

Just as Tyrone and Vanessa get upstairs to the bedroom the doorbell rings.

Tyrone says to Vanessa: "Who in the hell is this' it figures the one night I'm trying to do something nice for my wife, someone would interrupt us again, first the phone, now the door." Tyrone walks back downstairs and answers the door but he has an attitude. "Who is it?"

"Hi, Tyrone it's me Vikki."

"Hello Vikki, how are you?   How can I help you?"

"I'm doing good. I wanted stop by and introduce you to my friend Antonio."

Tyrone slaps him five.   He says to Antonio, "Good to meet you man, please forgive me I was just trying to have a romantic evening with my wife."

"We're sorry, but it will only take a few moments, can we come in?"

"Sure come in. Only for you Vikki, am I allowing you to interrupt a nice evening with my wife."

Vikki really doesn't care about that, because she thinks Tyrone has a motive behind this anyway.

"Tyrone honey, who is that at the door?"

"Your shadow, who else?"

"Tyrone now that's not nice; it's true but not nice." "Pleased to meet you. So Antonio, you seem like a

good man, my friend speaks very highly of you. Don't hurt her."

"I will make sure that I won't."

Tyrone says to Antonio "Don't. Even though she's a pest, she's like family and I will come after you, if you break her heart."

"I promise you I won't, and we really have got to go."

"Bye guys."

Vanessa says "Bye you two."

"Antonio looks so familiar. I know I've seen him before. He looks like this baller I've seen come to the office? Nah, I doubt it though. Okay Vanessa where were we?"

"On our way upstairs!"

"Let's go."

"I'm right behind you, handsome."

"Vikki, they seem like cool people, I've seen Tyrone somewhere before, but I can't quite put my finger on it."

"He's a very well-known and successful investment banker; he deals with clients who are multimillionaires."

"I thought I knew him, he's handling one of my accounts. I don't like to let people know what I do for a living, but since I'm with my future wife, I am going to tell you. I am a professional athlete, and that's how I know Tyrone, I had to do business at his firm, I don't think he remembers who I am."

"Oh, it's like that, I'm scared of you."

"Don't be scared. Just let me love you like a man should."

"Well that's fine by me."

"Antonio I'm glad that you are in my life. I pray that I make you as happy, as you have made me."

"Vikki I'm in love with you, it doesn't get any better than that."

CHAPTER SEVEN

"Hey baby girl how are you feeling, I'm up for round two."

"I'm okay Michael and I bet you are up for round two. Boy you can't handle all this good stuff."

"If you throw it this way, I will and can catch it. You want me to show you."

"No that's okay. I believe you I must say I didn't think anything was going to come out of this, but something just might. I can't believe that two friends became business partners, and are now falling for each other."

"You have probably been hurt by some dudes in the past, but believe me, there are still some good men around who know how to love a woman, and I am one of them."

"I see your mother taught you well, it's about time there are some good men in this world Lord, and please let me have one of them."

"Baby you got me and I'm not going anywhere, I'm a one woman man, and never forget that and we will be okay."

Kayla is feeling guilty, because she never thought that she would have feelings like this for Michael and for Tyrone; she has to make up her mind.

"Believe me Michael, I do understand, and I'm grateful." Kayla realizes that she must leave Tyrone alone, otherwise she is going to mess up a good thing with a good man.

"I will talk to you later, I have to wrap up some business, love you girl. I'm a blessed man."

Kayla is feeling a little sad, thinking out loud.   "How am I going to break it off with Tyrone?" *I have been with him for so long, but he is a married man, and God is blessing me with someone who is single. Lord I trust you so I'm going to do my best to stick it out with Michael.*

Michael is calling, "Kayla, Kayla. Is something wrong?"

"Oh, I'm sorry I didn't hear you, did you want something?"

"I left some papers on the desk, and I need them."

"I'm sorry Michael, here they are. I had something on my mind."

"I can tell, are you sure you are okay?"

"Michael, I'm fine just fine. I love you and I will see you when you get here tonight, don't be late. I will be waiting."

"Oh you can definitely bet that I won't keep you waiting."

As Michael leaves Kayla's condo Tyrone decides to call.

"Yes Tyrone, how are you today?"

"You sound like you don't want to be bothered."

Kayla pauses before she speaks. Finally she says to Tyrone, "I am okay; I just have a lot on my mind. I'm just trying to get ready for work."

"Something is wrong and I can hear it in your voice, this is me Kayla, now what's going on with you?"

"Tyrone, I said nothing is wrong, I'm okay, I'm trying to prepare for a meeting that has been stressing me out, that's all."

"If you say so, but I don't believe that for one moment. So why don't we get together this evening?"

"Sorry, but I can't. I don't know what time this meeting is going to be over, it's going to be a doozy."

"I'm not happy about this but I have to live with it, I will speak with you later." Tyrone hangs up the phone with an attitude. He decides that he is going to call his wife.

"How is my number one woman? Let's go to dinner tonight, just the two of us."

"I would love that. I have one more thing to wrap up and then I will meet you. By the way where are we going?"

"To that little Italian restaurant, the one you like on Groove Street,

Chez Anthony's something or another."

"I know what you are talking about, it sounds great. I love that restaurant."

"How is seven pm?"

"Seven o'clock is fine and it's good to be able to spend some time with my husband. Tyrone, are you sick?"

"Why in the world would you say that?"

"Because this is the second most romantic thing you did for me this week."

"You act like I don't do things."

"Well, I'm going to be nice."

"Yes, be nice before you get in trouble."

"That's what I'm hoping for, to get into plenty of trouble. What about you try-guy?"

"Don't you mean "Fly-Guy?"

"No, I mean "Try-Guy."

"Girl, have you been smoking, what in the heck is a "Try-Guy?"

"You figure it out."

"Now you know you are wrong, see you in a bit darling."

Tyrone doesn't really want to go to dinner with Vanessa, but he has no choice since Kayla has decided that she won't be able to meet him.

"Well hello Michael this is your business partner, how is the meeting going?"

"Quite well, we got the account so I thought that we would go out and celebrate."

"Great, I would love to go out. I'm actually on my way out the door; I'm wrapping up this meeting. I'm glad that you got the account. I will tell you all about what happened at the meeting. I will meet you at the restaurant; by the way Michael where are we going?"

"I would love to go to that Italian Restaurant on Groove Street, Chez Anthony's."

"Michael I don't think that's the name, but I know what you are talking about. I will see you there about seven fifteen."

"Kayla baby you've got a date, see you there. I can't wait."

"Neither can I, let me get off this phone so I can run home and change into something more appropriate. Love you."

"And Kayla, I love you as well."

Tyrone and Vanessa both walk into Chez Vous, and are waiting to be seated. After waiting for over five minutes the Maitre'd finally comes over to seat them at two of the best seats in the restaurant.

"Honey wow this is really nice, you out did yourself on this one."

"Only the best will do for the lady in my life."

"Tyrone Tyler, did I tell you how much I love being your wife?"

"And I love being your husband."

"I know you don't believe this but I do want to have children, and I believe that it's going to happen.   I will do whatever it takes."

"Let's not worry about that, at least not right now. Let me enjoy you."

As soon as Tyrone says that; Michael and Kayla enter the restaurant. Michael has his arm around Kayla's waist they look more like lovers than just business partners.

As they are walking to their seats Michael spots Tyrone. He asks Kayla, "Isn't that the guy who you closed the deal with the other night?"

"Yes it is Tyrone Tyler and I believe that's his wife."

"Kayla let's go and say 'hello;."

"No Michael, let's not; they look like they want to be alone."

"But Kayla, it doesn't hurt to say 'hello'."

Tyrone notices the two of them together.He motions to them.

Tyrone says, "Hello you two, what brings you two here?"

Michael says, "Well I won a big contract, so I wanted to take the woman whom I will eventually share my life with to dinner to celebrate."

"Well where is she Michael?"

"She's here, I'm talking about Kayla."

Kayla is stunned she didn't expect Michael to say that in front of Tyrone.

"Tyrone who is this lovely lady you are with?"

"This is my wife Vanessa. Vanessa, this is Michael Thomas and Kayla Jones."

"I've heard so much about you both, especially you Kayla. We must get together for lunch sometime."

"Oh, I would really love that, here is my business card. Call whenever you like. I would love to talk."

Tyrone, is mad and feeling uncomfortable at the same time.

Vanessa asks both Kayla and Michael. "Why don't the two of you join us?"

"Thank you, but no thanks, I want to enjoy this time with Kayla while we can."

Vanessa says, "I do understand, well enjoy your meal."

"Vanessa why did you invite them to our table? I want to spend this time with you."

"Tyrone please do not make a big deal about this.   I'm sorry my mistake. Can we just enjoy the rest of the evening?"

"Fine Vanessa and I didn't mean to snap at you."

"It's perfectly okay. I'll let it go this time," Vanessa says sarcastically.

Michael and Kayla kiss. Tyrone is livid, because he sees his mistress with another man, and they are kissing in front of him. He wants to jump across that table and kick Michael's behind, but he knows that he has to play it cool. Now is not the right time to get indignant.

"Kayla seems so nice and I like her business partner, I actually think they make a nice couple, don't you?"

Tyrone is in a daze, he barely hears what Vanessa is saying. "What! Did you say something sweetheart?"

"Yes I did, I said that I think Kayla and Michael make a nice couple."

"She is already spoken for."

"She may be spoken for now, but things can change; and who knows he might treat her better than the person she is with."

Tyrone is totally in a whole new world.

"Tyrone to earth, have you heard anything that I said to you?"

"I'm sorry I heard you, just thinking about something. Can we change the subject, and talk about something else?"

Tyrone is so upset by what he sees with Kayla and Michael that he wants to leave the restaurant, he doesn't even want dessert. He motions to the waiter for the check. He goes to pay the bill, but all the while he can't but wonder about the situation with Kayla and Michael. Tyrone will make it his business to call her later. Upon exiting the restaurant, Vanessa says good bye to Michael and Kayla; however Tyrone barely says one word. "Tyrone aren't you at least going to say "Good-night?"

"Honey, I don't have to say a word."

" Tyrone now that is very rude, what has gotten into you?"

"Nothing, now just get in the car so we can go home." They arrive home in record time Tyrone was so distracted by Kayla and Michael that he has basically ignored his wife. She is so bothered by Tyrone's attitude that she tells him she is tired and heads straight to the bedroom. She doesn't even give him a peck on the cheek.

"Tyrone, I have a busy day tomorrow; they need me to take over some projects, so I won't be home at the usual time."

"Yeah me too, I have to meet with a new client that I am trying to pursue. Good night. What do you mean you won't be home at the usual time?"

"Tyrone not tonight, I can't with you. Good night."

"Vanessa we will see about that. I'm too tired to argue with you, we will discuss this tomorrow." Tyrone is up earlier than usual, that's because he tossed and turned all night, thinking about Kayla.

Vanessa is about to leave the house when Tyrone asks her what time is she coming home. "Honey I told you last night that I didn't know. I'm late as it is. I will talk to you later."

Tyrone tries to block Vanessa from leaving. "Woman, I want to know what time you are coming home."

"Tyrone, I repeat we will not have this discussion. I don't know what time I will be home."

"If you can't tell me what time you're getting home, then I think you need to quit."

"I will not quit." She tries to push Tyrone aside, to little avail.

"Woman I know you are crazy. You need to be home by seven and that's an order."

Vanessa is livid. "Good bye Tyrone, I will see you when I get home."

He grabs her by the arm, "seven o'clock!"

Vanessa leaves without saying a word.

Tyrone screams "Woman, I mean it and don't you ever walk away when I'm talking to you!"

Vanessa totally ignores her husband; somehow she manages to open the door and leaves.

Tyrone is spinning out of control, he realizes that he must get a hold of himself. After his screaming match with his wife, he takes a deep breath and decides that he wants to talk to Kayla. He needs to find out what's going on, especially because he didn't like what he saw last night.

Kayla's phone is ringing.

She answers, "Hello, how may I help you today?"

"Kayla this is Tyrone, we need to talk."

"I know who this is, and what is it that you want to talk about?"

"You know what about, I'm coming over there right now."

Tyrone rushes over to Kayla's; he is basically at her office before she can hang up the phone.

"Have a seat, and now what seems to be the problem rick-a-shay rabbit. You rushed over here like…" Before Kayla can say another word, Tyrone lashes out at her angrily.

"You know what the problem is, explain last night."

"Tyrone what happened last night?"

"Look woman, don't act stupid! I want to know what that was about last night."

"Tyrone, what in the world are you rambling about?"

"Dammit! I'm talking about that kiss between you and Michael."

"It was just a kiss and what's it to you?"

"You are my woman, and I don't appreciate you flirting with other men in my face."

"Give it a break Tyrone, I was having dinner with someone who is truly interested in me, and who is single."

"I don't give a damn, you are not to see him or anyone else for that matter. Do you understand what I'm saying?"

"Tyrone don't take that tone with me. You are the one who is still married, playing games with me and your wife. Don't get upset because there is someone else in the picture. You had your chance to take this relationship to another level, but you chose not to. So if someone else is interested in me, I guess you are going to have to deal with it and remember, Michael is my business partner."

"And from this day forward make sure that is all you two are. I will be keeping a tab on you. I want to know who you are with, where you are, what time you are arriving and leaving, when you get home, and how you are getting home."

Kayla bursts out laughing. "Negro you have lost your mind. Don't get it twisted, you have no say so in this relationship, my name is not Vanessa."

"And what the hell is that supposed to mean? Kayla you don't know who you are dealing with, I will hurt you."

"How dare you threaten me please leave my office now!" Kayla slams the door behind Tyrone.

Tyrone is so upset that he doesn't notice Michael at all.

"Hey babe, what is going on? I just ran into Tyrone, and he acted like he didn't know who I was."

"Oh it's nothing, he is upset because I told him that we might have to go in another direction on our deal and he isn't so happy, I tried to explain that he still has our business, but he might have to be a co-banker; and either he does it or it's not a deal. I told him I'm not budging on it, and he has forty-eight hours to decide. He's mad because his commission will be cut slightly."

"Oh well, then he will just have to get over it, on to something better. How is my favorite girl?"

"I'm great now that you are here, can we leave? I've had a stressful day, as you can see; and all I want to do is go home and relax."

"That's all I needed to hear from you, let's go."

Michael and Kayla are listening to soft music, and are about to enjoy each other's company when Kayla's phone rings.

Kayla says hello and realizes it's Tyrone on the other end. She so wants to hang up on him for the way he acted at her office today.

"Before you hang up the phone on me, please let me apologize for the way that I acted; but I really need to see you. I do love you and I want to try and make things right with us."

"I'm sorry but I can't; maybe we can meet tomorrow. Good-bye." This time when she hangs up she cuts her phone completely off so that she and Michael will not be interrupted again.

"Babe who was that?"

Kayla lies to Michael; she hates to lie to him, but what else could she say. "It's Trudy from the office, she needed me for something; but I told her that I was unavailable and that I would speak with her tomorrow. Now where were we?"

"Come closer, now close your eyes and let me give you a massage. How does that feel?"

"Michael that feels like heaven!"

"Wait here for a minute I'll be right back."

Kayla is stunned that Michael leaves the room "Michael what are you doing?"

"Baby, please keep your eyes closed."

"Michael is preparing a romantic evening, with rose petals, candles and a nice bubble bath."

"Michael you are scaring me, what are you doing?"

"Look, please give me one more minute keep your eyes closed. I'm almost finished, okay now you can open them."

"Oh my goodness Michael, I can't believe you did this for me. I think I'm going to cry, what am I going to do with you?"

"Just love me with all your heart and I will love you unconditionally, forever and ever, always this. I promise to you."

"Michael, I promise you that I will love you with all my heart; but promise me that no matter what, you will always be there with me and for me."

"I will be there for you and with you. I will be by your side through thick and thin, for better or for worse, for the good days and the bad days. Through it all, I am totally yours."

"Now Michael, that just made this evening more special than it already was. I know that you are truly the one for me. I truly thank God for you." Kayla wants to end this nonsense with Tyrone and commit to Michael, and she is going to break it off with Tyrone, sooner than later. She doesn't want to put Michael through this mess; he deserves so much better than what she is giving him now.

"Michael just hold me." He happily obliges. What a nice way to end the evening in his arms, in bed together. They both fall asleep in each other's arms. It's a nice Friday morning, both Michael and Kayla are getting ready for work. Kayla is happy as can be. She has an incredible business and an even more incredible man. What more can she ask for? She is singing to herself. I am blessed over and over again. Michael is smiling at the love of his life, he's happy because she is happy with the relationship. Michael beats Kayla getting dressed, as usual. He kisses her on the forehead on his way out the door. As he leaves she calls Tyrone, not because she wants to see him but because she really wants to break it off with him. She knows it's going to be hard because Tyrone is not the type of man who will just let you walk out of his life. She knows that she is taking a chance, but this is something she really has to do. She calls Tyrone hoping that he doesn't answer the phone.

He picks up "Hello. Is this the woman of my dreams?"

"I don't know about that, but it's me Kayla."

"Kayla, I know who you are. How are you?"

"I'm fine Tyrone, how about dinner tonight? Is seven thirty okay with you?"

"That should be fine."

"I'll call you later and let you know where to meet." "Okay Kayla babe. I love you."

"Talk to you later, Tyrone."

He is puzzled by her response, but he is not going to
say anything to her until they meet in person.

CHAPTER EIGHT

"Hey Vikki how is it going, I don't see much of you now that you have this new man in your life."

"Vanessa what can I say, he is wonderful, but I'm still skeptical."

"He is really into you and he is a good man, stop being on the offense. If God has blessed you with someone who wants to treat you like the queen you are, then let him. I'm waiting for wedding bells."

"Vanessa now you are getting ahead of yourself. I just want to take things nice and slow."

"Don't take it too slow. Be nice to Antonio, okay future Mrs. Anderson. I like that it has a nice ring to it."

Vikki chuckles, "Girl it does, doesn't it. By the way how is Tyrone?"

"He has been moody lately, this job is really getting to him, the other night we got into a heated argument because I told him that I didn't know what time I was getting home. He had the audacity to tell me that if I wasn't home by seven pm then I would have to quit my job."

"What did you tell him?"

"I told him that he was crazy and to move the hell out of my way."

"Well what happened next. Vikki I really don't want to talk about it. Just know this, I'm still working; and at this point there is nothing that he can say or do to me. I can't sit home and do nothing and he's going to be upset when I tell him I am registering to go back to school tomorrow, even though he said that I couldn't before. I have to do what is best for me and my career."

"Vanessa, I know what the problem is, he wants children and he's frustrated."

"I know, and I feel bad. I have been to doctor after doctor and yet nothing has happened."

"Vanessa, I have a friend who was in the same situation as you are. She was unable to get pregnant and someone referred her to a specialist. I will call her for you tomorrow if you don't mind and get the information for you."

"I don't know. I will let you know. You know, what harm can it do? I will do whatever it takes to make my husband happy."

"So Vanessa, have you heard from Kevin lately?"

"Not too loud Tyrone is upstairs. Yes I've heard from him and we are going to meet tomorrow after I register for school."

"I'm so proud of you that you are going back to school, so when are you going to tell Tyrone?"

As Vikki says this, Tyrone walks into the room.

"Tell me what?"

Vanessa is skeptical to say anything so she lies when she sees him and says to him "it's nothing honey."

"It's something, so tell me what it is. I'm waiting."

"Well Vanessa, that's my cue. I will see you tomorrow, good-bye Tyrone."

"Bye Vikki. By the way how are things with you and Antonio?"

"Things are great I really have to go, talk with you later. Vanessa, I'm praying for you."

"What is she praying about Vanessa?"

"Listen, you have been stressed out and I really don't want to bother you with my life.

"Your life is my life, so tell me. We can stand here all night, but you are going to tell me."

"Okay, I'm going back to school. I register tomorrow."

"No way! I don't think that's a good idea now."

"Tyrone, what is wrong with you? This is a wonderful opportunity for me to get my Bachelor's degree. I put my career on hold because you asked me too, and now that I want to do something for myself, you are denying me this opportunity. I don't believe you."

"You won't be home, and coming home all times of the night."

"For the record, I only need two more classes and I will obtain my degree; please let me do this, and only one of the classes will be at night, it won't interfere with us. Plus I just got some good news."

"You know what just forget it. Vanessa begins to walk away Tyrone grabs her."

"And what good news did you receive?"

"Vikki is going to refer me to an in-vitro specialist. So now maybe you can have that son that you always wanted. Honey, aren't you excited about this?"

"Yes," Tyrone says unenthusiastically. He wants children, but not with his wife. He can't seem to get his mind off of Kayla, especially because he now knows that there is someone else who can possibly take his place.

"Honey where are you? Did you hear what I said?"

"Honey, I'm sorry, I heard you and I am excited."

"You sure don't act like it."

"I'm good, I'm sorry if I seem distracted, I'm not feeling well. I'm going to go to bed." Tyrone kisses Vanessa on the forehead.

"Tyrone wait, we can go to bed together, maybe that will make you feel better."

"Yeah! That might make me feel better. Tyrone is lying through his teeth."

After a night of rest, Vanessa is not feeling so happy; she can't believe that her husband wouldn't hold her in his arms again. She is trying her best to be a good wife, but she is at wits end. She is on her way to Desire's to get prepped up for her dinner date with Kevin.

Delicious says to Vanessa, "Hey girl, come and sit down and tell a sista what's going on."

"Well I have a dinner date tonight, and I need to get my hair done."

"Is it with that fine Mr. Milk Chocolate Kevin?"

"Yes it is, but it's just dinner."

"Vanessa girl you need to stop. Girl let me tell you, he and I would have dinner, dessert and a night time snack. As a matter of fact he might be the night time snack." Delicious laughs out loud.

Vanessa tells Delicious to stop being nasty.

"I'm not nasty I'm just greedy, and Vanessa you need to give him some, otherwise Milk Chocolate will be melting in my mouth and hands."

Shaniqua works at Desire's and she is a friend of Delicious; she is trying to get Delicious to be nice. "Will you please behave, Delicious. All that talking, now I'm getting excited. I'm going to pray."

Vanessa tells Delicious and Shaniqua. "The two of you are both a hot mess."

"Okay Vanessa, let's dish the dirt."

"Nothing to dish, my husband doesn't want me to go back to school to finish my degree and every time I mention it he wants to pick a fight."

"Now that's hard to believe. Tyrone doesn't seem like the type of man to pick a fight, especially when he feels so strong about education. Do you need me to convince him for you?"

"No thanks Delicious, I think I can handle it. I'm sure he will say yes, he's been under stress lately."

"Tyrone might be under stress, but I would love to be under."

Before Delicious finishes his sentence, Vanessa says, "Delicious get your mind out of the gutter."

"Girl, my mind wasn't in the gutter, it was in something else… ha ha."

Shaniqua jokingly says to Delicious "You need help." And then she turns to Vanessa and says to her "You know what that sounds like don't you?"

Vanessa says, "No I don't, and I bet you are going to tell me."

"Girl, did you forget our last conversation "control issues" starting arguments. He is definitely creeping on you."

"I don't think that's it, if it were he would have said yes I could go back to school."

Shaniqua says to Vanessa "Girl wake up, your husband is playing you and doing someone else, it is what it is. Do you need a reality check? Vanessa he needs to feel that he has power over you, and you are falling into his trap. If you want to go back to school, just do it. Believe me Vanessa, he will get over it so fast his head will spin."

"Vanessa, I'm with Shaniqua, you have to stand up for yourself. If you are going to register for school, then do it. Tyrone will be mad as hell at first, but I bet you after a minute he will welcome it."

Vanessa asks Shaniqua "Do you think he will be okay with it?"

Shaniqua says, "Girl trust me, he won't be at first but eventually he will be okay with it. Just do it."

"Shaniqua, that is definitely easier said than done."

"Speaking of done Vanessa, I'm all done. How do you like your hair? Now let me know what happens tonight with Kevin.   Girl, milk chocolate and nuts, woo I want to touch that."

"Delicious, you are too funny, see you later." Vanessa calls Tyrone. She tells him that she will be home about nine-thirty tonight and that she loves him."

"Thank you Delicious, I can always count on you to make me look fabulous."

"I wasn't trying to listen to your conversation with your husband, but I think nine-thirty is too early, that's not enough time to eat anything if you get my drift." (laughing)

"Boy you want me killed. Tyrone will kill me for sure if I come home later than that. He's a clock watcher."

"A clock watcher, I'm sorry I thought you said a cock watcher, now that would be interesting."

"Good bye Delicious. Lord help him please!"

"Good bye Shaniqua and thanks again for listening. See you both soon."

"Bye Vanessa, and it was my pleasure."

"Delicious, I feel sorry for Vanessa."

"Shaniqua, why do you feel sorry for her?"

"Because she is so naïve, she really loves her husband and she can't see that he isn't the one for her. Now she really needs to talk to that Kevin guy he would make a good husband for her."

"Shaniqua stay out of my head because, I was just thinking the same thing. Tyrone is going to mess up eventually, just wait and see."

"Tyrone is listening to the message that Vanessa left. He thinks this is a good opportunity for him and Kayla to get together, since they haven't seen each other in a couple of days."

"Hey Kayla, it's me Tyrone. Vanessa is going to be home about nine-thirty tonight and I thought that we could get together. I'm really sorry about the other night and I really need to see you, please call me back."

"Hello Tyrone, it's Kayla.   I received your message. I can come see you, but I won't be able to stay for a long time."

"Whatever you want Kayla, I promise no pressure at all."

"It's six o'clock now I will see you in an hour. Take care."

"I'll be waiting for you my love."

Kayla arrives at the Tyler residence, but her heart is no longer in this relationship. She has finally found someone whom she really likes and she is getting fed up with Tyrone and his games. She rings the bell, she tries to put on a front.

"Hey Kayla babe, come inside."

"Hello Tyrone, how are you this evening?"

"You look beautiful, as always."

"Why thank you for the compliment. I appreciate that."

Tyrone goes to give Kayla a kiss and she turns from him.

"Kayla honey, I know that I said some things that I should not have said, but we all say things when we are upset. You don't know how much I want to be with you and I promise you that I am going to fix this situation so that we can be together."

"Tyrone please stop with the lies; you have been saying that for the past five years and you haven't done a thing yet. Do you think that I am that stupid? You are never going to leave your wife, and I'm okay with it. Why don't you just let me go, and stop playing with my feelings!"

"Kayla I am going to leave her, five years ago I was just starting out in the business and I am now at a point in my life where I am financially able to leave my wife and she will be able to live comfortably. I'm sure you understand that."

"I do understand, but I'm not feeling this or you anymore."

"Baby, just hang in there with me a little while longer, I promise this will all be worth your while."

Kayla doesn't want to be bothered with Tyrone, but he manages to kiss and caress her. She is vulnerable.

"Tyrone, will you stop it before we do something that we really shouldn't be doing."

"What is it that we shouldn't be doing?   I'm sure you want this as much as I do."

"I really don't think we," Kayla drifts off.

"We shouldn't what?   Just let me make love to you." They are trying, getting it on, but Kayla stops Tyrone and tells him, "Only if you use a condom."

"Use a condom, woman please."

"Kayla what do I need a condom for? You only use a condom for one or two things, plus I hate them; but I will do this only for you." As they are attempting to make love Tyrone realizes that it's about eight fifteen, he tells Kayla that she has to leave because Vanessa will be home any minute now.

"I know you don't want to hear this now and I don't want you to leave, but Vanessa will be home soon."

"Tyrone this is exactly the stuff I'm talking about I'm gone." Kayla gets dressed in a hurry.

"Babe please understand. Give me a little while longer, and I will sit her down and let her know that I'm no longer in love with her, just think about it for me."

"I am done, delete my number." As of this moment Kayla is no longer interested in Tyrone's lies, she realizes that Michael is now and will always be the man for her. "Tyrone I don't care what you do, I am so finished with you. I have to go and be with a man who wants to truly be with me."

"Kayla I'm not hearing anything that you are saying, so stop with the foolishness and give me a kiss."

"Good Bye Tyrone.   What part of I'm done with you don't you understand?"

Tyrone knows that he has to do something or else he will lose Kayla and he doesn't want that at all; but he has to find a way to break the news to Vanessa. Either way someone is going to get hurt in this.

Vanessa arrives at home a little earlier than usual she says "hello" to her husband, but Tyrone is distracted because he is thinking about Kayla and Michael and how he knows that he could lose her to him if he hasn't already.

"Hey babe how are you doing?"

Tyrone doesn't hear a word Vanessa is saying.

"Tyrone, I said how are you doing? Okay something is wrong, do I need to take you to the hospital because this is the second time that I have spoken to you and you seemed like you were somewhere else. Tyrone, do you hear me?"

"Babe I'm sorry, what did you say?"

"Is there something wrong with you? You seem like you are not here mentally."

"Vanessa honey I'm sorry, I'm okay. It's just that I was trying to bring in a new client, and I thought they were going to say yes, but now it seems as though they might go with another company, and they were a multi-million dollar client."

"Tyrone where is your faith, you know that you are number one in your firm and you are the best at what you do. If you don't get this client that's okay, you have so much money it's ridiculous, and you will get other clients. That I am sure about."

Just as Vanessa says that, Tyrone's phone rings.

"Hello Mr. Smith, I didn't expect to hear from you, is everything okay?"

Voice on the other line is Mr. Smith. He is a Senior Partner at Tyrone's firm. "I just wanted to say congratulations, Tyrone you got the account. Your commission is 5.5 million dollars; I knew you could do it. I would also like to talk to you about becoming a Partner in the firm."

"Thank you Mr. Smith, I really appreciate your calling me." Hangs up the phone. "Yeeeeeeeees."

"Honey what is it?"

"Who's the man?"

"You are, I guess? What happened?"

"That was Mr. Smith, one of the Senior Partners in the firm. That account I thought I wasn't going to get, I actually got the account; and because I did a good job I got a 5.5 million dollar commission and let me tell you the rest. They want to make me a Partner!"

"See, I told you to have faith I am so proud of you."

Tyrone grabs Vanessa by the arms and dances with her. "Vanessa, I truly thank you for all of your support." Tyrone wishes he could say to her that he is in love with Kayla. He knows he can't just yet, but he knows that he has to do it.

"That's what I'm here for, and I'm glad that you are a supportive husband, who doesn't mind that his wife is trying to pursue her degree."

"What, wait I really don't like the idea of you going back to school. it's bad enough you wanted to work when I said that I would take care of you, and when you said that you wanted to work longer hours I didn't like it. I let you do it anyway and I'm okay with that so far, because it hasn't interfered with the home; but I'm not sure about school because it means that you won't be home."

"Tyrone honey, I promise it won't interfere with us it's only two classes that I'm talking about."

Tyrone is hesitant but decides to say "Okay" to Vanessa. "You know what, it's only fair Vanessa; you support me in all that I do, so why shouldn't I support my beautiful wife."

"Thanks babe, you don't know how happy I am right now. I needed this. I love you so very very much. Yes, I'm getting my degree, thank you God."

"Look at you, you are really excited about this. As long as you can keep up with taking care of me and the household, then I'm good."

Vanessa gives Tyrone a long and passionate kiss.

Tyrone asks, "what was that for?"

Vanessa says that it's for being such a wonderful husband, despite the fact that she can't give him children. "Tyrone, you are a wonderful husband. And I thank you so much for this, I won't let you down. I can't wait to call Vikki and tell her my good news."

CHAPTER NINE

Vikki's doorbell rings and in walks Antonio. "Well hello Handsome."

"And hello to you, Gorgeous, you are looking quite well today."

"I'm actually on my way out the door.   I have an appointment at the hair salon would you like to come with me?"

"Salons are not my thing but I will take you there."

"Well thank you, that is so nice of you."

"No need to thank me, that's what a man is supposed to do for his woman; now come and give me some sugar."

"Antonio, you need to stop otherwise I won't be able to get anything done. We will have time for that later."

"Damn, damn and damn woman, if you only knew what you do to me."

"Then we will do it when we get back, whatever it is," Vikki says, chuckling.

"Baby, you ain't said nothing but a word."

Vikki arrives with Antonio.   She wants him to come in and meet the gang.

"Antonio, this is Shanqiua and Delicious."

Antonio astonished says "D Who?"

"Delicious, I can say it nice and slow for you. DDDEEEELICIOOOUS."

"Delicious that's enough, you are scaring Antonio."

"It's okay, I'm fine but why do they call you Delicious."

"Because one taste of me and you will see why. You are one fine caramel candy cane."

Antonio says, yelling, "TMI TMI and TMI."

Vikki reminds Delicious that she came to get her hair done. She knows what it's like when you miss your hair appointment with Delicious.

"And what are you here for, Caramel Candy Cane?"

"I'm only here to drop my lady off.   Vikki call me when you are finished and I will come and pick you up."

"Delicious says to Antonio "You can pick me up and down anytime you want to."

"See you soon."

Delicious says, "I hope so."

"Delicious, he's not talking to you."

"I know, he doesn't have to talk to me if he just listens. I'm okay that. I will do the rest."

"Delicious, you are a pure hot mess."

"You got one out of three correct.   I'm hot, never been pure and I will mess someone up if I need to. So Vikki, how long have you been seeing Antonio?   He seems to be sweet on you."

"He is a sweetheart, and I actually like this guy; we have been dating for all of seven months, and I like being with him. Usually the guys that I meet turn out to be jerks after the first few months but there is something special about Antonio."

Shaniqua says to Vikki "Girl if he makes you happy then I'm happy for you; he better not hurt you, otherwise I will snatch him black."

"That's right girl, he will go from being a caramel candy cane to caramel pudding." Delicious laughs out loud.

 "Stop it you two, but it's good to know you have my back."

Shaniqua says,"you know us girls have to stick together."

Delicious says to Shaniqua, "That's right, we girls sure do need to stick together. Vikki is there something special that you want me to do?"

"I'm not sure, just something that's cute and nice.

Let me see what I can do for you. Here is the perfect hairdo for you, go sit under the dryer for about 10 minutes. I can have this done for you in no time."

"That's why I love coming to you, you are the best."

"Why thank you. Please excuse me while I take this call. This is Delicious how may I help you? Look here, I don't know anything about that sorry boo, but he was at my house last night, and he will be there again. Don't hate now don't call my phone again or there will be problems."

Vikki asks Delicious, "Is everything okay?"

Delicious says with anger in his voice, I'm okay, just a little man situation… nothing I can't handle. Your hair should be dry by now. Okay let me get you out of here. I know you want to get back to that handsome man of yours."

"Are you sure you're okay?"

"I'm cool, why are you still asking me that?"

"Because my hair is not completely dry, and that's not your style; you usually make sure that I'm bone strait."

"I'm going to blow dry it today, and I'm sorry for snapping at you, I'm cool but when I get home it's going to be something."

Vikki says to Delicious "Please don't cut anyone. I don't have any money to bail you out of jail."

"Girl, I hear you I promise I won't. I'm not going to jail for anyone. Just let me put the finishing touches on your hair. Ladies can we please change the subject?"

Delicious asks Vikki the million dollar question. "So where does Antonio work?"

"I'd rather not talk about that; the most important thing is that he treats me good and I'm happy. I haven't smiled like this in so long. But I still have my guards up."

Delicious says to Vikki, "Girl, you are so right, if he makes you happy then that means, more than anything else, be good to him. I know you haven't been serious with anyone in such a long time, but let him love you up. Vikki there comes a time in your life that you have to let your guards down. I can tell that Antonio really wants to be with you wholeheartedly you can tell by the look in his eyes. I bet you two will be engaged soon."

Shaniqua asks, "Engaged in what?"

Delicious says, "Engaged with each other."

Shaniqua asks Delicious, "Who's engaged with each other?"

Good help and normal people are so hard to find - Antonio and Vikki, that's who Shaniqua."

"Antonio is my boyfriend and Delicious thinks that he and I will be engaged soon."

Shaniqua now asks Vikki, "what are you and Antonio going to be engaged in?"

"Girl, just forget it. You know common sense is a flower that doesn't grow in everyone's garden."

"Vikki, no need to explain. I'm with you on that one. There's no help for some people."

"So are you just about finished with my hair? I'm not trying to rush you or anything, I'm just saying…"

"Yes I am actually done with your hair, and so how do you like your hairdo, does it pop for you or do you want something else?"

"Yes it pops for me. No I don't want anything else, this is perfect I love it because it's so different from my usual hairdo, take a picture; you know you can make a girl look good."

Vikki's phone rings. It's Vanessa on the other end, "Hey girl, what's going on?"

Vikki when and where can we meet? "I want to pick up some shoes, we are celebrating."

"Celebrating what?"

"Girl I will tell you when I see you. I should invite Kevin to go with us."

"To go shopping Vanessa? I don't think so, girl. Kevin will stop talking to you for sure, especially when you go shopping for shoes. I think we need to do this by ourselves." Vikki chuckles. "Well I'm about to call Antonio and tell him to pick me up from Desire's. I'll have him take me to Nattie's and we can talk then."

"Okay girl, see you in a few."

"Okay Vanessa, I will see you later."

"Thanks Delicious, that was Vanessa and she is in a happy mood."

"How do you know that?"

"Because she said she wants to celebrate, and whenever she is in a good mood she wants to go shoe shopping, that's how I know. And that means we can be shoe shopping for the rest of the night. Plus she always buys me a couple of pair. Gotta go, I will talk to you later."

"Stop by the receptionist and make an appointment, see you in a couple of weeks. Bye girl, love you."

"I have to call Antonio and let him know that you are finished." Vikki proceeds to call Antonio.   Antonio arrives but he doesn't want to come inside of Desire's.

"Hey baby, I'm outside the salon."

"Why are you outside?   Come inside the salon."

"That's okay, I'm good standing out here."

Vikki tells Delicious, "You scared my man off. Now he doesn't want to come inside the salon."

He might not want to come inside Desire's, but I have somewhere for him to come. Ha ha."

"See you later guys. I'm gone."

CHAPTER TEN

Kayla is lying down on her bed she isn't feeling well, but she doesn't want to alarm Michael.

Michael calls out her name "Kayla baby where are you?"

"Hey Michael, I'm upstairs lying down."

Michael asks Kayla "What's wrong?"

"I was dizzy, so I decided to leave right after the meeting."

"Why didn't you call me and let me know, are you okay do you want to go to the hospital?"

"No honey, it's not that serious I didn't want to bother you. Oh by the way, I want you to know that the meeting was successful before I could leave they called me and said that we have the account, so I snagged not one, but two new clients."

"Baby, that's great, but I would have filled in for you. The next time something like this happens, I expect you to call and talk to me."

"Okay Michael, I will do that next time."

"I'll be back, I'm going downstairs to finish up some work."

"Kayla baby, are you hungry?"

"I am kind of, but I don't want to put you out of your way."

"Look woman, you are not putting me out of my way… that's what

I'm here to do. I'll be back shortly I'll go to the store to get some things."

As Michael proceeds to leave the house, Tyrone calls Kayla. He wants to stop by and see her.

"Hey Kayla, it's me babe. I miss you and I want to see you. I have so much to talk to you about."

"I know who it is. Not tonight, Tyrone, can we do it some other time?"

"What do you mean, not tonight some other time?

Do you have a man in your house?"

"Look Tyrone, Michael was here; he just went to the store."

"What is he doing in your house? You know I don't want that man in your house. I don't know what it is but there is something going on between the two of you."

"For the record Tyrone, I fainted today so I came home to lie down and when he didn't see me come to the office after my meeting he became concerned so he came by to check on me to make sure that I was okay. Now he is getting me something to eat. Look I'm in no mood to argue with you. I will speak to you later."

"I'm sorry babe I didn't know you weren't feeling well. Are you okay? Do you need anything from me?"

"Yes Tyrone I need for you to call me another day. I'm really not in the mood to talk. Like I said, I will speak to you later."

"Okay, love you, bye." Tyrone is feeling slighted.

"Good bye and good night." Kayla realizes she can't sleep, she decides to listen to her head phones. She doesn't hear Michael when he comes in the door.

"Hey baby I'm back, Kayla I'm back." Thinking that something is wrong with Kayla, Michael rushes upstairs. "Kayla thank God you are okay."

Kayla is startled "what's wrong Michael what happened?"

"Nothing now. When you didn't answer, I thought that something had happened to you."

"I'm okay, I was just listening to some music, I'm so hungry."

"How is this" Now scoot over some."

"Michael, what are you doing?"

"I am here to take care of you and to make sure that you get better. Is that okay with you?"

"Michael, you know that's why I have fallen in love with you."

"Kayla, I fell for you the first time I laid eyes on you. I knew you were the one for me. And that still hasn't changed."

"Michael I am so glad that you are a part of my life, I will cherish this always." Deep down Kayla knows that she has to break away from Tyrone.

"Come here woman and give me a kiss."

"But Michael, I'm not feeling well. I don't want you to catch my cold."

"There is no other person I would rather get sick from than you. I am willing to catch your cold, but most of all I want to catch your heart. Are you ready for that?"

"Michael I'm ready to give you all of me and in more ways than one. I love you dearly."

"And Kayla, I feel the same way. I know who my soul mate is."

"Now lie down and get some rest. I will be down stairs if you need me. Love you girl."

CHAPTER ELEVEN

Vikki asks Vanessa "Girl how did you get away from Tyrone?"

"It wasn't easy. I lied to him and you know that I don't like to lie to my husband. Something has been going on with him lately, he seems so distant."

"Vanessa, did you ask him what all that was about?"

"Yes I did. He says it's the job, Vikki."

"That might be true, but there has to be something else. Talk to him and find out what's really bothering him."

"Well I know that he doesn't want me to finish school, so that might be it."

As Vikki is about to say something, Kevin walks into the restaurant.

Vikki asks Vanessa, "Why doesn't Tyrone want you to go back to school? Especially because he knows that this will help your career."

"He feels that my home life will slack that I won't be there for him that much.   I explained to him that it's only two classes, and that I have supported him through everything and he should support me."

Kevin is finally able to get a word in edge wide "Hello ladies, you both are looking quite lovely. He kisses Vanessa on the cheek."

Vanessa says to Kevin, "Well thank you and you are looking quite handsome yourself."

Vikki being nosy, asks, "Kevin, what made you stop by the restaurant?"

He tells her that he was actually in the area and that he had just finished a meeting and decided to get a bite to eat.

Vikki sarcastically says to him, Boy, you know you saw Vanessa in here and that's why you stopped in here. Kevin, you can't fool me."

Just as Kevin is about to say something, Delicious strolls in.

Kevin is thinking to himself *Oh! Lord why me. I wonder what Delicious is going to say out of his mouth now.* "Well, if it isn't Milk Chocolate himself! Waiter, can you put him on the menu as the special of the day?"

Vanessa says to Delicious, "Boy, what is wrong with you? Sit down."

I'm just saying, "He is one Doggie Bag I would love to take home."

Kevin tells Delicious thanks, but no thanks.

" Once you had GAY. You will forever stay! Let me stop messing with you. So fancy running into you guys tonight."

"I just needed a little down time from home, Tyrone and all the other stuff."

Kevin says to Vanessa, "So you're still not being treated like you should."

Vikki responds, "Yeah, her husband is not too keen on her going back to school, even though he reluctantly said "Yes" he really doesn't want her doing anything but satisfying him. He is a total control freak. I really can't understand what the resistance was all about. Tyrone knows good and well you will be able to handle both school and home."

Delicious has to put his two cents in, "I know you don't believe me but my DIVA radar is telling me there is more to it than that; and believe you me I will find it out sooner than later."

"Listen up you guys, it's not that at all. Tyrone's been stressed out and he just found out that he is going to be a partner in his firm; so that's just more stress on him."

"Girl, I know the perfect way to release his stress; you bring that man of yours my way and when he gets back home he will be stress and worry free, or shall I say Delicious free."

"No thank you Delicious, I can handle my husband. I have my own method of releasing his stress."

"But just in case, Vanessa, I'm letting you know. Delicious is here to help you out in any way that I can."

"You know Vanessa, I really hope that things don't work out for you and your husband."

"Now why would you say that to me, Kevin?   That's not nice at all. I'm trying to save my marriage."

"Because I'm slowly falling in love with you and I know that you can do better.   Sure you have wonderful houses, nice clothes, shoes and fancy cars, but do you have "True Love"?"

"Yes, I have true love."

"Vanessa, I truly doubt it. If you had true love, your husband would never deny you from furthering your education. He would not ask you to stay home so that you can always take care of him and the home. See a true love would know that a woman can take care of her home, man and career, and never let any of them fall. But most of all a True Love will never take you for granted."

"Girl, I know I have a true love and his name is Antonio Anderson. Now what about you Vanessa, do you really have a true love or what?"

"Wow, maybe I don't have a true love."

"Vanessa, there is no need to fret. I don't mind being your true love so when you are ready for a true love or shall I say a true man like me, Kevin Keys, then all you have to do is call me."

Delicious, trying to be funny says, "If she won't call you, I definitely will."   You can be my true love, new love and a boo love."

Kevin leaves the restaurant, and as he leaves he responds by saying, "Have a good day ladies and Delicious."

Vikki, Vanessa and Delicious All say, "Good bye true love." They all chuckle".

"Vanessa, I don't know about you, but I think that man is really digging on you. You can hear it in his voice and he smiles so much that he is showing all the teeth he doesn't have."

"Vikki, now you know that wasn't nice to make that comment about his teeth; you are too funny. I know that he really likes me, but I don't want to break his heart. I'm a married woman."

Delicious loudly says in front of Vanessa, "An unhappy married woman, I feel in your spirit."

"Vanessa, why don't you give the man a chance? No one said it had to be intimate, you can have a friend that you can always talk to."

"Vikki, I really have to think about it. This will be something new and different for me."

Delicious laughing, voices his opinion to Vanessa.   "Girl try it, you might like it, I know I would."

"Well, you two, I have to get home.   Tyrone just left me a message that he is on his way home so maybe we will arrive at the same time."

"Bye girl, and remember what your true love said.   Either way, Delicious and I got your back Vanessa, I love you sister girl."

"Bye Vanessa, I will speak with you sometime tomorrow. I'm going home too I can't wait to see Antonio."

"Vikki, call me tonight so we can talk. Now I really have to go, I don't want Tyrone to start fussing because I'm not there when he is. Love you sister."

"Girl, my true love is coming over and I don't plan on calling on anybody but two names, Antonio and Jesus, if you get my drift."

"Vikki I don't want to let on but I know for sure Tyrone is cheating on Vanessa. Vikki honey, a man that cheats is often a man who is controlling, he wants to keep tabs on you so that you can't blow up his spot. He's cheating, and mark my word. Iwillfindout.com. Believe that."

"He is not cheating on Vanessa, and for the record, what would make you think that? Delicious, please don't say that.   Vanessa would be so heartbroken, she has fought hard to make this marriage work. Just imagine loving someone who doesn't love you the way you should be loved. She is hurting because each day she is being tormented with the fact that she can't give her husband children. And if Tyrone is cheating on her and she finds out about it I know that it will shatter her whole world. Vanessa already thinks that she is less of a woman because she can't have kids. Do you know what this would do to her emotionally and mentally?"

"Wait ,wait, wait! Tyrone is not controlling and he is not cheating, so let's get that out of our minds now."

"Vikki if you say so, I'll let you think that."

"Delicious, I need to school my girl on this."

"Nope, you need to leave it alone. I could be wrong and I don't want to be the one to break up an already unhappy home."

"Bye Delicious, I'm leaving."

"Vikki, you can't leave without me."

 "Okay, then let's blow this joint."

"Vikki this isn't what I want to blow. Oops did I say that out loud?"

"Yes, you did… loud and clear for everyone to hear."

Vanessa finally arrives home. Tyrone is there already. "Hey honey how was your first day in your new position?"

"It was hectic, so much responsibility. I'm so tired."

"Honey do you want me to whip up something for you to eat?"

"No that's okay, I am actually too tired to eat. I'm going to take a shower and head straight to bed."

"Honey, are you sure?"

"Yeah I' m sure. I will see you when you come to bed."

"Okay, I just want to finish some paperwork. Love you."

"The same here."

Vanessa is sitting on the couch thinking about what Kevin has said to her about a true love, *Lord why in the world am I thinking about that man?* As she sits quietly thinking about Kevin, her phone rings. It's Kevin.

Vanessa is whispering "Hey Kevin how are you?"

"Vanessa I just wanted to hear your voice and to let you know that I miss you and I will be waiting for you for as long as it takes."

" Thank you but I really can't talk because my husband is upstairs; but maybe we can finish this conversation tomorrow."

"How about lunch tomorrow? We can meet in a neutral place and so that we won't seem suspicious invite your friend Vikki. Is that okay with you?"

Vanessa still whispering says "That's fine, but I must go."

As Vanessa is talking, Tyrone comes downstairs to check on her.

Vanessa tells Kevin good night.

Tyrone wants to know who is on the other line.

Vanessa startled by Tyrone, "Oh it was only Vikki."

"If it's Vikki then why were you whispering on the phone?"

"Because you know that sometimes Vikki and I can get loud on the phone, especially when we are talking girl talk and I didn't want to bother you."

"Yeah that's definitely true, but it's not a bother."

"Honey, I thought you were tired."

"I can't sleep. So I came downstairs to get some water I have a headache."

Honey, now you know you shouldn't take medicine on an empty stomach; please eat something before you take that medicine. If you don't want me to whip up something, can I at least put something in the microwave for you?"

"Darling, you don't have to go through all of that."

"Look Tyrone it's not a problem I'll nuke you something and you can take it upstairs. Oh by the way I just wanted to let you know that I start my first class tomorrow."

"Tomorrow! Why so soon? I was thinking about that… maybe you should put it off for a little while longer."

"Tyrone I'm too tired to argue with you about this. I'm not going to put school off any longer. I am starting tomorrow and that's final; I want to finish sooner."

"Vanessa we are going to talk about this some more."

"Not tonight, we won't. It's already a done deal. Please let's not go through this again. Now she is really thinking about what Delicious said "Controlling"."

"You know what? You are absolutely right, you go and get your degree." Tyrone realizes that this will give him more time to spend with Kayla if Vanessa is out of the house.

"Did you just say that I was right? Am I hearing you correctly?" Now she knows that something isn't right.

"Yes, you heard me. I said it's okay to get your degree. I have no right to hold you back. I don't care."

"You don't care." Knowing that this might lead to a blowup Vanessa quickly changes the subject. "Oh by the way before I forget to mention this to you, Antonio wants to know if you want to go to a basketball game."

"Sure do!" Tyrone asks, "Who is playing?"

"I think he said that he had third row seats to the Knicks and the Lakers on Friday…"

"Heck yeah, I'm down for that. How did he get such good seats?" Tyrone heads upstairs to the bedroom. He looks at Vanessa and says, "I'll be waiting."

"Oh, you ain't said nothing but a word."

"Tyrone honey, Antonio is a professional athlete. Don't you know what team he plays for? He only plays for your favorite team, the Los Angeles Cougars."

"Cool, that's what's up. I knew that he looked familiar, he is a star running back on that team. Vikki went and snagged herself a baller, I didn't know she had it in her."

"Honey, I am right behind, you but let me call Antonio and tell him you want to go." Vanessa calls Antonio.

"Hi Antonio, this is Vanessa. I spoke to my husband, and he said that he would love to go to the game with you on Friday."

"Good tell him I'll stop by his office on Friday, and he and I can have drinks before the game."

"I will let him know. Take care."

Tyrone calls out for Vanessa.

"I'm coming, give me a minute. Here I come."

"Woman what took you so long? You know how I get."

"And if you keep bothering me, you might not get none!" Vanessa isn't really joking. She would rather make love to Kevin, than to have sex with her husband.

"Woman, do not play with me like that."

Vanessa tells Tyrone that Antonio will stop by the office on Friday so that you guys can have some drinks before the game and by the way I haven't started playing with you yet. Vanessa laughs playfully.

Although Tyrone is lying in bed with his wife, he wishes that it were Kayla who was next to him. He is drifting off, thinking of ways to tell Vanessa that he is no longer in love with her and that he wants a divorce. He can't bring himself to make love to Vanessa, so he pretends that he is sleep.

"Tyrone honey, come and let's play doctor." Vanessa notices that Tyrone is not responding to her advances. When she turns around she realizes that Tyrone is knocked out. Vanessa is hurt, but she isn't heartbroken. Day by day her feelings for Tyrone are diminishing.

It's early Tuesday morning. Tyrone is up before the crack of dawn.

Vanessa wants to know why he is up so early. He should still be in bed sleeping.

Tyrone tells Vanessa that he has a ton of work to do and that he has three meetings that he must attend, since he is now a partner in the firm.

"Honey, you know what's funny? You didn't want me to back to school because you thought that it would keep me away from home, but it looks more like you are the one who will be away from home."

"I know and I'm sorry, but it comes with the territory. I would love to sit and talk to my darling wife, but I really have to be going."

"Tyrone, you have a good day. I love you, and be safe."

"Honey I love you as well, peace out." Tyrone can't wait to get out of the house. He is so focused on making things right with Kayla that deep down he doesn't care if both of Vanessa's classes are at night, as long as he gets to see Kayla. Vanessa can do whatever she wants.

Tyrone is praying that he hasn't lost Kayla, especially not to that Michael character.

Tyrone decides to contact Kayla, but her phone is going into voice mail. Tyrone doesn't know that Kayla turned her phone off because she doesn't want to be interrupted. She is with Michael the man of her dreams.

"Hey Kayla baby, how are you feeling today?"

"Hi Michael I'm feeling a little better today, I still have a slight headache, but I will be okay, I'm going to stay in bed for a few more moments, then I am going to get ready to go to the office."

"Ms. Jones, you don't need to come in remember I have everything under control."

"Okay Michael, but are you sure?   It's just a headache and I'm sure that I can make it in. And what's with the Ms. Jones?"

"Baby, I'm just being sarcastic, that's all. You need to stay home and get better. I will see you later this evening and I want you to call me if need anything. As a matter-of-fact, I will call and check on you."

"Michael you're the best, that's why I love you so much."

"Anything for my girl, love you baby. I'll see you later tonight." Michael walks out the door.

Just as Michael leaves the house Kayla's phone rings, it's Tyrone

"Hello Tyrone how are you doing?"

"I'm good darling. How are you feeling today? I know that you were not feeling the best last night."

"I'm doing better, I still have a slight headache. I decided that it would be best not to go into the office today, so I'm going to rest and relax. Michael said that he would call to check on me; he is such an incredible man."

"Wait a minute Kayla I didn't call you to hear you talk about another man. I thought I made it very clear that I didn't want you talking to him."

"Tyrone, in case you forgot. I think I can talk to whomever I want to. Remember, you are still a married man." Kayla is feeling nauseated she runs to the bathroom and throws up.

Tyrone is concerned he can hear Kayla throwing up on his end of the phone. "Kayla are you okay?"

"I'm fine, look I will talk to you later." She hangs up on Tyrone.

Tyrone is feeling upset, he decides he is going to surprise Kayla. So he rushes over to her house. He is ringing her door bell like he is crazy.

Who in the world could this be? I'm not expecting anyone. Kayla opens the door with a slight attitude; she is in no mood to be bothered with anyone right now.

"Tyrone what are you doing here?"

"I was already in the area, so I decided I would come by to check on you and to talk to you about this thing you got with Michael."

"There is nothing to talk about. I'm not feeling well. I have been throwing up the past couple of days."

"Girl, are you pregnant?"

"I doubt it very seriously there is no way that I am pregnant. I took a pregnancy test and it was negative. It is probably some food that I ate the past couple of days that didn't agree with me. Anyway, what are you doing here?"

"I wanted to stop by and see you."

"Now you see me and now you can go."

"I'm not leaving I came to make sure that the future Mrs. Tyler was feeling better. You know Kayla, that really sounds nice."

"Yeah, I guess so."

"Kayla, what do you mean… you guess so?"

"Tyrone I'm sorry, I'm just not feeling well; so I'm in no mood to talk with you or anyone else for that matter.   I just want to get back in my bed and sleep. Is that too much to ask for?"

"You know what? I'm not liking this situation.   I'm only leaving because you need your rest, but we will get together tomorrow… believe that."

"Okay Tyrone, if you say so. Just go please, so I can get some rest."

As Tyrone leaves, Kayla closes the door behind him. She can't help but wonder if she really is pregnant, she can't be. She decides to call her doctor.

Lord, I pray that I'm not pregnant; but if it turns out that I am pregnant please let it be Michael's baby, I mean Tyrone's baby. What am I talking about? Michael is a good man, but Tyrone will be a good provider and so will Michael. But I'm sure that Michael is not ready for children just yet. Well only time will tell… I will know in a couple of days, if I'm pregnant. "JESUS HELP ME PLEASE!"

"Hello Dr. Simpson, this is Kayla Jones. I need to come and see you right away, it's urgent. Is it possible for you to fit me into your schedule? I'm available to come and see you today, if at all possible."

"I don't usually see patients on a short notice, but if you can get here in the next thirty minutes, I will help you the best way I can."

"Thank you, Dr. Simpson. I will see you in a half hour."

"I'll be expecting you, Kayla."

Kayla arrives at her doctor's office almost out of breath.

"Hello Dr. Simpson."

"Hello Kayla, why are you out of breath?"

"I basically ran here so that I could be on time. You said to be here in a half hour."

"You didn't need to go through that. If I wasn't able to see you at that time I would have made a way to see you before the day was out. How are you doing? It's been a while since I've seen you. So what brings you in today?"

Dr. Simpson I have been throwing up the past few days.   I took a pregnancy test, but it came back negative. I just want to make sure that I'm not pregnant."

"Here is your cup you know what you need to do. Once you have finished, please give the cup to the nurse and have a seat in the waiting area."

"Thank you doctor I pray I'm not pregnant. Oh my GOD, what if it's Tyrone's baby? Oh please don't let me be pregnant."

Dr. Simpson summons Kayla "Please come in to my office."

"Well doctor, please give it to me straight. Am I pregnant or what?"

"Yes, the test was positive, you are pregnant."

"I am Dr. Simpson? Are you sure? I guess you are, wow I'm pregnant. Thank you Doctor." Kayla doesn't know if she should be excited; then she realizes that she slept with Michael, so this could be his baby. *Michael will be so happy, at least I hope that he will. I have to find a fun way to tell him.*

Okay I've got to find a way to tell Michael… hmm. Jesus please help me. Okay I'll go to the office and let him know. Nah, I can't do that, he's busy. Kayla takes a deep breath. *I will tell him when he gets home.*

Michael calls Kayla on the phone. "Hello Kayla baby are you okay?"

"Umm, yes Michael I am okay, why do you ask?"

"Okay Kayla, what's wrong?"

"Michael, who said that something was wrong?"

"Kayla, you know that I can hear it in your voice when something is wrong. So what is it?"

"Honey, I don't want to talk about it over the phone I will talk to you later tonight. I love you." Kayla hangs up the phone before Michael can say anything else.

Michael knows that something is wrong with Kayla, he is puzzled about the conversation. He decides to leave the office because he is bothered that Kayla has something to tell him and he doesn't know what it is.

Michael races home in his car to find out what is wrong with Kayla.

"Kayla baby, I got here as soon as I could. Would you please tell me what's wrong."

"Michael why did you leave work? I said that I'm okay. You didn't need to cancel any meetings to come home, it could have waited."

"Kayla you are hiding something from me and I want to know what it is, and I want to know now."

Kayla, still in shock that she is pregnant is in a daze. She is scared that

Michael will leave her if he finds out they are having a baby. She ignores Michael.

"Honey what in the world is wrong with you? I'm not leaving here until you tell me what's wrong with you."

"I'm so scared to tell you because you might hate me for this."

"Girl what in the world are you talking about? Stop talking in riddles and tell me what's wrong."

Kayla takes a deep breath and begins to say to Michael the following. "I didn't want to have to tell you this way I wanted it to be in a different setting."

"Oh my GOD, just stop. I think I know what it is that you are going to say, you are trying to break up with me."

"Michael honey, what in the world are you talking about? All I wanted to say is that I'm pregnant and I was scared to tell you because I thought you would be mad at me."

"You want to run that by me again, you are what?"

"I was scared to tell you because I thought that you would be mad at me."

"No, the part just before that."

"That I am pregnant?"

"Kayla. are you absolutely sure?"

"Yes I'm sure, I went to the doctor today and she confirmed it. I'm so sorry. I know you don't want a baby and I didn't mean for this to happen. If you want me to get rid of it, I do understand."

"Woman are you crazy? I'm going to be a father and you better not even think of getting rid of my child. Do you realize how happy that you have made me?"

"You mean, you aren't mad at me?"

"Mad at you? No not at all. Why in the world would I be mad? I have waited for this moment for a long time and I prayed that you would be the one I have a child with.   I know this might not be the right time and you might say 'no', and now is as good a time as any to ask you so here it goes. Kayla Will You Marry Me?"

"Michael I don't want you to propose to me because you feel that you have to because I'm pregnant with your child."

"Baby girl, what you don't know was that I wanted to marry you from the moment I laid eyes on you. I knew that GOD had blessed me with my soul mate, all this did was speed up the process. So you still never answered my question."

"Your question… oh the marriage thing. Yes Michael, I will marry you!"

"Well alright, a wife and a baby! I'm a blessed man. Michael is smiling and trying to cut a step with his new fiancée. We can go and pick out your ring tomorrow. I'm going to be a father, now that's what I'm talking about. God is so good!"

"Michael are you sure you're okay with this? You do know what this means… mood swings, long nights and late night feedings?"

"Kayla, I'm good right now. So I'm going to have a Michael Junior."

"Excuse me! It could be a girl, as a matter of fact I know it's a girl."

"To tell you the truth, I don't care what we have as long as we have a healthy baby."

"Michael, I totally agree with you on that, now can we please get some sleep? I have had a very long day, and I want to get to the office early tomorrow."

"And Kayla my love, just one more thing!"

"Yes Michael, what is it?"

"I love you more now, than you'll ever know."

Kayla is praying that this really is Michael's baby and not Tyrone's baby.

It's early Monday morning, Kayla is up and ready to get an early start on the day. She is already dressed. She looks at Michael who is half asleep and says, "Michael honey, I'm leaving for the office. I will see you when you get there."

"Kayla, wait one minute. You're pregnant and you don't need to worry about anything I will take care of your meetings."

"Michael, please don't treat me like that. I am capable of working. It's just a meeting, I can handle this." Before Michael can say anything else Kayla is already out the door.

"Kayla get back here!" That woman sure knows how to wreck my nerve. In the middle of Michael getting dressed, he starts making phone calls. He shifts some things around on his calendar then he calls Kayla.

"Kayla, I shifted some things around. Can you meet me about twelve o'clock noon so that we can go to the jewelers?"

"I will see you at the office at noon time." After Kayla hangs up the phone with Michael she gets another call it's Tyrone.

"Hello Tyrone, how are you doing?"

"Hey sweetie, I'm calling to find out how you are doing. You sound much better today."

"I'm doing better."

"So did you go to the doctor to find out what was causing you to throw up?"

"Yes, I found out what the problem was; but I don't want to talk about that right now."

"Why not, aren't I supposed to be your man? So you should be able to talk to me about anything."

"Well this is not the kind of thing that I need to talk to you about over the phone; it should be done face-to-face. Tyrone is there something else that you want?"

"Kayla, you know you have been acting real bitchy lately and I want to know what's up?"

"Can I talk to you about this at another time? I have a quick meeting to go to and then I have an appointment at twelve o'clock. We will talk about this in person, I promise. Talk to you another time."

Tyrone is yelling on the other end of the phone.

Kayla has already hung the phone up. She heads to her meeting

CHAPTER TWELVE

Tyrone is pacing the floor, he decides to call Kayla. Upset that he has to leave a voice mail message on her phone. "Kayla, I really need to talk to you can you come over here?"

Kayla returns Tyrone's call, she asks Tyrone "where is your wife?"

She is at the hairdressers she won't be back for at least another two hours.

Kayla is on her way to Tyrone's house, she realizes that she has to inform Tyrone that she is pregnant. She doesn't want him to know that there is a chance that Michael might be the father.

The doorbell rings, it is Kayla.

"Hello, babe it's good to see you, I have missed you so much. Now tell me what is going on with you? You have been acting funny toward me."

"Tyrone, we need to talk and I don't think that you are going to like what I'm about to say to you."

"Kayla dear, you are absolutely right, I'm not going to like this if you are sleeping with Michael. I am going to rip his head off."

"Wait a minute do I have to remind you once again that you are a married man."

"I don't care, I'm in love with you and I want to be with you."

"Yet you are still with your wife. Look, let me just say this and be done with you and this craziness. When I went to the doctor today, I found out that I am pregnant."

"That's great babe, now we can be a family."

"Are you crazy? How can you think that we can be a family, when you are still with your wife. Tyrone, I am going to raise this child without you."

"Kayla you must be crazy. Tyrone, I am not crazy and I meant what I said. You are the one who is crazy, you are still with your wife, and trying to play me after all these years. I'm raising this kid on my own. No I'm not crazy. You are the crazy one, you are carrying my child and you think I'm going to let you just walk away and not have any input in my child's life. I don't think so."

"Look Tyrone it's over, there is nothing you can say or do that will make me want to continue in a relationship with you. I can raise this child all by myself. Please Tyrone just stay with your wife and leave me and my child alone."

"Kayla it's not over I'm going to leave her."

"Tyrone, please stop selling me false dreams, they cause way too much pain. I am out of here." Just as Kayla is about to leave Vanessa comes through the door.

"Tyrone what in the hell is going on here? Why is this woman in my house?" And don't say she is here to drop off papers for you to sign. That story played out a long time ago."

"Vanessa, this is Kayla Jones."

"Why does that name sound familiar? Aren't you the woman from the restaurant?"

Yes, I'm also an attorney. Your husband landed an account with me and my business partner. I was just leaving."

"Kayla wait!" Tyrone races to the door before Kayla can open it. "Vanessa, Kayla is my mistress. I have been having an affair with her for the past five years."

"Tyrone, you want to run that by me again? She is your mistress, and you have been sleeping with her behind my back all these years, how could you?"

"Vanessa I'm so sorry, I didn't mean for this to happen. I met Kayla five years ago, and what started out as a friendship turned into a meaningful relationship."

"Sorry, you are right about that; you are a sorry ass Negro. I don't believe you. I want you out of this house and I want you out now."

"Hold the hell up Vanessa, this is my house too and I'm not leaving, I worked hard for this house."

"Wait a minute, I want the both of you to listen. Tyrone you first, you are so right.   I fell in love with you and I felt bad about being in a relationship with you because you were married; but you told me that you weren't happy in your marriage because your wife could not give you the kids that you wanted.   You promised that you would leave your wife, but you never did, you kept me like a puppet on a string. And now your secret is finally exposed. I'm glad that your wife finally knows how much of a creep you really are. I thought that you were the man of my dreams, but I have realized over the course of five years, you are not that man. I thank GOD that he has blessed me with someone who wants to be with me totally and completely and things are good between him and me.   Vanessa, you deserve so much better. I am truly sorry, I didn't want this to happen and I definitely didn't want you to find out like this. I told Tyrone time and time again to be honest with you and let you know what was going on, I'm so sorry that it had to end this way."

"Tyrone this is it, I'm leaving. I am gone for good."

"Kayla, you are not going to walk away and not let me have a part in my baby's life."

"Watch me Tyrone."

"Excuse me, wait right there you mean to tell me that she's having your baby. I don't believe this. Vanessa starts laughing to keep from crying. You know what Tyrone I can't stand to look at you. You are lower than scum. I'm leaving, this marriage is over. I can't wait to divorce your no good trifling behind."

Kayla and Vanessa both head out the door leaving Tyrone standing in the house by himself, looking dumb and stupid.

Vanessa is putting on a brave front, she definitely doesn't want the other woman to see her crying. Vanessa is in her car wondering where in the world she went wrong in this relationship.   So many emotions are running through her mind that she can't think straight. She wants to go back in the house and kill Tyrone, but what would that prove? Not a damn thing. One thing for sure, that asshole is not worth spending time in jail. Vanessa realizes that she has to get it together, she has to figure out where she is going. There is only one person in this whole world she can talk to and that's Vikki.

Vanessa arrives at Vikki's house, She is knocking on her door and ringing her bell. Vikki screams out as loud as possible. "Who in the world is ringing my bell like they have lost their mind?"

Vanessa crying asks "Can I come inside?"

"Girl sure, what in the world is going on, what happened? Did something happen to you? Tell me something please is Tyrone hurt?"

"Vikki, I just found out that Tyrone has been having an affair with the attorney Kayla Jones for the past five years of my marriage."

"What! Oh honey, I am so sorry.   Now you know I don't have a problem going over there and breaking the windows out his car. You just say the word. And it's done."

"What am I doing? I'm so sorry for bothering you. I hate that you have to see me like this."

"Girl there is no need to apologize. You are my friend and you know that I will always be there for you."

"I'm not finished telling you the best part, she is pregnant with his baby. Vikki, my marriage is over just like that."

Wait! You mean to tell me that this chick is having his baby, yet he didn't have one with you? You know what, I don't think that Tyrone had a problem with having a baby he didn't want one with you because he was with someone else. That low down dirty dog. Girl you ought to sue him for everything he has and then some."

"Vikki, what are you doing?"

Girl, I am contacting my attorney. Vanessa we are going to get through this together."

"Vikki, I don't want to intrude but can I please stay here for a couple of days?"

"Now you know that you can stay here as long as you like."

Vanessa cries herself to sleep on Vikki's couch.

The doorbell rings it's Antonio.

"Hey baby girl how is my sweet sexy thing doing?"

"Shhh, you are talking too loud. And I am doing okay."

"Shh nothing. Who in the hell is in this house? Girl, I will bust a cap in someone. Where is he?"

"Antonio, what in the world are you talking about? Do you think that I would be crazy enough to have a man here, let alone open the door so you can kill us both? It's not like that at all. Vanessa is here."

"Oh my bad! What is she doing sleeping on your couch?"

"She and Tyrone had a big fight. It seems that Tyrone has been having an affair for the last five years of their marriage and to top it off the woman is pregnant with his baby. Vanessa is not handling it too well. The things Tyrone put her through."

"My bad you're a good friend to let her stay here. Damn this means I can't get any."

"Sure does, please try and understand."

"I don't like it, but I understand. See you tomorrow. Bye baby."

Vanessa says sarcastically, "Bye Antonio."

"Girl, I thought you were sleep."

"I was. I had to say something to keep me from crying again. Vanessa starts to cry again anyway. I can't believe my husband cheated on me. Thinking back Vikki, I remember the day that I had to set the alarm and saw a strange woman in my house. Looking back I should have put two and two together then, and realized that something was up between her and Tyrone; but I didn't want to think that my husband of twelve years was being indiscreet in our marriage."

"Vikki, that tramp was in my house."

"Vanessa are you sure?"

"Oh, I'm sure alright. Some things you never forget. I never believed for one moment that she was just dropping off papers to Tyrone. He was always defensive whenever I mentioned anything about cheating. He made me think that I was crazy, and that he loved me, but all the while he was doing someone else."

"That Negro has lost his mind. Well it's on, and he better be ready because he is going to lose everything."

"Don't worry about anything. I got you on this one."

"Vikki, I don't know how I'm going to make it."

"Listen girl, you are a strong woman and we will get through this together; now please go to sleep we will talk in the morning."

"Thank you so much for letting me stay at your house. You are truly a good friend and I appreciate this and I'm so sorry about tonight."

"What are you sorry about? You didn't do anything, Tyrone did."

"Yes I did. I interrupted a romantic evening with you and Antonio."

"Girl, don't worry about it. Believe me, there will be other romantic evenings… trust me on that one. You sure you don't want me to break a cap off in Tyrone? Because you know I will."

Vanessa chuckles, "Girl I'm good, let's just get some rest."

Antonio decides to make an appearance at the Tyler residence; he is upset by what has happened between Tyrone and Vanessa. He rings the doorbell.

Tyrone answers, "Who is it?"

"It's Antonio, man."

"Hey Antonio, what brings you by so early in the morning?"

"Tyrone I need to talk to you. I stopped by Vikki's house last night and I saw Vanessa lying on her couch. I'm a little upset by the fact that you cheated on your wife."

"Look brother, I haven't been happy in my marriage for a long time and I wanted to tell her, but I didn't know how."

"Man up brother. It's not nice to play with someone's feelings like that, leading them on. You put that woman through some hell and you know you are going to have to pay for it."

"I know and I am sorry for the way things went down."

"And then you got this other woman pregnant. Now you know, that's a slap in the face to your wife. Tyrone, my brother, I used to respect you. Now I don't know what to think. It's brothers like you that make it hard for women to trust a real true man like me. You know the more I stand here and talk to you the angrier I'm going to get, so I think I just better leave before I say something that I shouldn't. But I will say this to you. That was a real punk move."

"You know what Antonio, you are right. I think it is best that you leave before we both say things that we shouldn't say, so step." Tyrone is angry at the way things went down, but he needs to settle things with Vanessa and try to make amends.

Tyrone calls Vanessa he leaves her a message on her voice mail. "Hey there, it's Tyrone can you please call me back? I really want to sit down and talk with you. I know you don't want to have anything to do with me and I understand that, but I want to apologize and see if we can come up with a divorce settlement that would be sufficient for you; and by the way, I love you Vanessa."

Next he calls Kayla. "This is Tyrone, please pick up the phone, I need to speak with you. I have been trying to talk to you since last night and I haven't heard a word from you. I will try you again. I won't stop until I get a hold of you."

Kayla finally decides to call Tyrone back, he has called at least ten times. "Tyrone why are you calling me? I don't have anything to say to you. It's over between us. When are you going to realize that? There is no me or you. Do me a favor stop calling me if you don't, I am going to change my number."

"Kayla honey what do you mean, it's over between us? It will never be over between us you are carrying my baby."

"The only thing that we have in common is this baby. I am in a relationship with someone else. And he is going to raise this baby."

"Who are you in a relationship with? And you have lost your mind if you think that I am going to let some other man raise my child as his own. Not happening, not in this life time; so whatever you been smoking, stop because it's affecting your sense of thinking. It is making you talk crazy."

"Tyrone I am in a relationship with Michael we have been seeing each other for quite a while now and I am happy with him. So please let me go and let me work it out with him."

"Kayla I can't lose you or my baby."

"Too late Tyrone, you already lost us and this time for good. Goodbye Tyrone."

Tyrone angrily slams the phone down.He knows he has done wrong, but he refuses to give up on Kayla and his baby. He leaves his home and goes to work.

Vanessa decides to stop by her house to pick up some more clothes. She is hoping not to run into Tyrone.

Vanessa yells out "Hello is anyone here?" *Good he's gone let me get my things and get out of here.* Just as Vanessa yells out "hello", Tyrone comes back home realizing that he forgot some documents.

"Vanessa how are you doing? Look I just wanted to say that I'm truly sorry I never meant to hurt you like this."

"You're sorry, I doubt it! You made me feel that I was less of a woman because I didn't have your children. You are a punk, you don't know the meaning of true love. God you are so funny."

"What are you rambling about now?"

"You see I knew about your woman for quite a while, but I didn't want to believe it I allowed myself to think that there was nothing going on. But in the back of my mind, I knew that you and that Kayla chick were more than clients. Yet I supported you, I loved you anyway, yet I was never your true love. But you know what Tyrone, I don't care anymore I want a divorce now, and by the way I have a real TRUE LOVE and it definitely isn't you. I'll be back to get my things when you aren't around. You make me sick. You are nothing more than a coward."

"I'm leaving and I want you and all your things gone when I get back home."

"Well ain't this some stuff you're getting an attitude with me, and you are the one who messed up. You know what Tyrone you're not mad at me, you're mad because you got caught. You thought you could have your cake and eat it too. I'll be glad to leave this house and to leave you. Good damn bye." Vanessa slams the door behind herself after she leaves.

As heartbroken as Vanessa is she tries to muster up the strength to go to work. She wants to just take the day off to get her mind off this whole situation, but she needs to keep busy or she will have a nervous breakdown. She can't let anyone at the job know what's going on. She doesn't know how she will make it.

She begins to pray. Lord please give me strength to go forth this day, help me to stay calm and give me peace. My heart is heavy, but I know with you Lord I will be okay."

Vanessa decides to call Kevin. " Hello Kevin this is Vanessa. I know it's been a while. I wanted to call to see how you were doing?"

"It's good to finally here from you. I almost thought you had forgotten about me."

"I didn't forget you at all, I'm just going through a lot right now. I'm headed to work, but I would like to get together with you soon."

"I will call you later tonight and maybe we can go out for dinner. How does that sound Vanessa?"

"Kevin it sounds like music to my ears. And Vanessa don't wait this long to call me again. I get hot every time I hear that sweet voice of yours."

"Thank you for that Kevin I really needed to hear that now. I will call you soon. You take care and have a blessed day."

"You too Vanessa. Bye baby."

"Same to you Kevin baby." Vanessa laughs.

Reality has set in that Vanessa has to speak to the divorce attorney. Never in a million years did she think that she would be doing this. "Hello this is Vanessa Tyler. I was referred to you by Vikki Black."

"Yes Ms. Tyler. I am Shaunice Johnson. I was expecting your call. I would love for you to come into my office so we can talk and start on your divorce proceedings. How about this afternoon does three o'clock work for you?"

"I'm sorry Ms. Johnson that's a bad time for me. How about six o'clock?"

"Let me check my calendar, give me one minute. You know, I have some space at that time, see you at six o'clock. Let me give you my address. It's Fifty Four Thirty West Seventh Street. I am on the second floor. I look forward to seeing you then."

"Thank you so much Ms. Johnson I will see you at six o'clock." After she finishes talking to Ms. Johnson, Vanessa calls Vikki.

"Vikki, I want to thank you so much for the referral for the divorce attorney. She seems like a good woman. How do you know her?"

"I met her through a mutual friend I have known her for almost three years."

"It's funny that you have never mentioned her to your best friend and why is that?"

"Vanessa there was really never a need. Plus that girl is so busy it's hard to catch up to her. Business must be slow because I haven't heard from her in about a month. I wanted us all to go out, but she never had the time. I am just glad that she was able to fit you in on such a short notice. She knows her stuff she is going to make sure that you are set for this life and the next life too." Vanessa and Vikki both laugh.

Kayla realizes how things turned out with Tyrone. She has to tell Michael that she was sleeping with another man while she was with him. She is hoping he will be okay with this, but she also understands if Michael decides to leave her once she tells him that she was with another guy. She thinks that she has lost Michael and now she knows or so she thinks she knows that she will have to raise this child on her own. She is torn because, at this particular moment, she doesn't know who her child's father is. This is some real mess.

"How is my favorite girl doing today?"

Kayla tells Michael, "You know that I love you and I want to be with you more than anything, but I have something to tell you."

"Baby, I don't know if I want to hear this, but whatever it is I'll have to take it like a man."

"I don't think that we should see each other anymore. I won't be coming back here anymore. I will come back later and get my clothes as soon as I can."

"Ok Kayla, what is going on here? Kayla I'm not liking what I am hearing from you. What is this all about all of a sudden you don't want to be in a relationship with me?"

Kayla is hesitant to say anything, but knows that she must tell him. "Okay Michael I didn't want to say this to you but I was seeing someone while I was also seeing you. Actually I started seeing them before I met you. I didn't think that I was going to fall in love with you while I was with them, but I did. I broke up with him the other day, and yes he is married."

"Wow that's a lot for someone to take in and my heart is hurting right now; but for the sake of our child I want us to be a family, and because I am so in love with you, I will forgive you this time for what you did. But if you ever do this again, I promise you that I will take my child and leave you in a heartbeat. Do I make myself clear?"

"Michael I promise you that this will never happen again."

"Kayla, I need to be alone right now."

"Whatever you need Michael. I really do want this relationship to work and I'm truly sorry for hurting you like this."

Kayla is talking to God. "God this baby has to be Michael's, it can't be Tyrone's. Kayla walks away feeling sad about this situation with the baby. Kayla has no one that she can talk to about this situation, or so she thinks that she doesn't. Some people will think that she is crazy for what she is about to do, but she was never one to care what other people thought of her. She decides to call Vanessa.

"Hello may I speak to Vanessa Tyler."

"This is Vanessa Tyler, whom may I ask is calling?"

"Vanessa this is Kayla."

"Kayla who?"

"Kayla Jones, please don't hang up. I know that I am the last person that you want to speak with, but I would really like to sit down and talk to you."

Vanessa is hesitant about meeting with Kayla, but she decides to do it because she wants to find out what Kayla had that she didn't have. "Okay Kayla, this goes against my better judgment, but I will meet with you. How about tomorrow?"

"That sounds fine can we meet at Chez Vous? Let's say about six thirty."

"Kayla that's fine. I will see you then."

"Okay, and Vanessa thank you so much for meeting with me. I really appreciate this. It means a lot to me."

Vanessa can't believe that she did this, but Vanessa was always a special type of woman. She always sees the good in people, know matter how good or bad they treat her. As soon as she hangs up with Kayla she calls Vikki to tell her what happened.

"Vikki are you sitting down? If you aren't, then you need to be because I have to tell you what just went down."

"You won't believe who just called me".

"Who Tyrone? What did he want, is he still lying, saying that he never cheated with Kayla."

"Believe it or not, Tyrone was not the one who called me, it was actually Kayla who called me."

"Vanessa you have to be kidding me. What in the world is Kayla calling you about?"

"Girl, she said that she wants to talk to me and I agreed to meet her."

"Vanessa please tell me that you didn't agree to meet with that woman."

"Yes I am going to meet her tomorrow at Chez Vous at six thirty."

"Vanessa aren't you afraid to talk to her? There is no telling what's going on in her head. I think you are going to need some reinforcement."

"Vikki I'm not walking around with any weapons."

"No girl, I mean taking another person with you. I will go with you. I want to make sure that she doesn't try anything. Better yet, I got it. Call Kevin and we both will go as your back up and we will sit at a table near you just in case. Does that sound fair enough?"

"Vikki she might be suspicious."

"How can she be suspicious?   She has never seen me or Kevin in person. We will act like a normal couple, having a nice dinner with each other that's all."

"Okay, I guess there is no changing your mind."

"Vanessa, I am not going to let you meet that woman by yourself; now call Kevin and set this meeting in motion."

"You twisted my arm, thank you so much Vikki. I really appreciate you. I'm going to call Kevin, let's just hope that he will be willing to go along with this plan."

"Vanessa. Girl Kevin is in love with you. I am quite sure that he will do anything for you."

"You are so right about that. I'm going to call him just as soon as I hang up with you, then I will call you back and let you know what he says."

"Okay I'll be waiting for your call."

Vanessa hangs up the phone, but not before telling Vikki to stay by the phone and make sure she doesn't fall asleep.

"Later Vanessa. Will you call Kevin and then call me right back. Don't have me waiting all night either. I know you Vanessa."

Vanessa dials Kevin's phone, she is getting butterflies in her stomach. She prays that the call goes to voicemail, but unfortunately it doesn't. Kevin answers the phone.

"Good evening this is Kevin, how may I help you?"

"Hi Kevin this is Vanessa."

"Hey babe, I didn't recognize this number. How are you doing?"

"Well I'm okay."

"Are you sure? You said that with slight hesitation in your voice is there something wrong?"

"Yes and no. I need a favor from you, but I'm not quite sure that you will be up to it."

"I'm listening. What's on your mind?"

"Well, I have to meet a woman by the name of Kayla Jones. She is a friend of my husband. She asked to meet with me, but she didn't say what she wanted to meet with me about. I agreed to meet her at a mutual spot."

"Okay where are you supposed to meet her?"

"At Chez Vous, tomorrow evening at six thirty p.m."

"So what do you need me to do, Vanessa?"

"I need you to be my reinforcement but there is a catch."

"Alright, just give it to me straight"

"Vikki is going to come as well and you and she are going to pretend that you are a couple having dinner. Vikki figured it would be good if the both of you were there while I talk to her. Kevin, I really can't go into details right now; but I promise you when the time is right you will know everything."

"Vanessa, I will do anything for you; but I just want to make sure that this isn't something dangerous or something that can get any of us in trouble."

"Kevin I promise you that it's nothing like that at all. You have nothing to worry about."

"Vanessa, you have a deal. I will see you and Vikki tomorrow night. Take care."

"Kevin, thank you so much. This is going to come as a shock to you, but I love you for doing this for me."

"You are welcome."

"Well I have to call Vikki and let her know that you are on board. Have a wonderful evening and I will speak to you tomorrow."

"Same to you Vanessa."

Vanessa proceeds to call Vikki to let her know what's going on.

"Hey girl what happened?"

"Kevin agreed to the plan. Believe it or not, I'm nervous."

"Vanessa what are you so nervous about? I don't think Kayla is stupid enough to do anything in a public place. Well girl, it's getting late. We will definitely speak tomorrow at least three or four times before we go to Chez Vous."

"You are right Vikki. I do have a job."

"See you later girl."

After a well-rested night. Vanessa heads to work she is feeling a little weird, she has not gotten used to not being in her house with Tyrone. She realizes that she has to take it one day at a time and eventually she will be better. Vanessa is looking at her schedule. With all that's going on in her life, she forgot that she has an appointment at six o'clock with the divorce attorney. What was she thinking that is so important? She doesn't have Kayla's number, she has to figure out how she can contact her and push their dinner back. *I got it, she is an attorney she must be listed. Let me find her firm on the internet. TJ Associates here we go, great I'll call her right now.*

"Hi Kayla how are you? This is Vanessa Tyler."

"Hello Vanessa how are you doing?"

"I'm doing okay. I'm sorry to have to do this but I forgot that I have an appointment at six o'clock that I can't cancel. Can we push our meeting back to eight thirty, is that okay with you?"

"Vanessa I'm actually glad that you called me because I wanted to call you and push the time back as well. See you at eight thirty."

"Kayla, thank you."

"No thank you, Vanessa."

They both say good bye to each other at the same time.

Vanessa calls Vikki. "Hey girl, it's me. I have to change the time for the meeting from six thirty to eight thirty is that ok?"

"That's fine Vanessa, but did something happen?"

"I forgot that I have an appointment with the divorce attorney at that time, that's all."

"How are you going to get in contact with Kayla to let her know?"

"Already taken care of. I called her, she is okay with it. But let me go because I need to call Kevin and inform him of the time change. See you girl."

Vanessa calls Kevin. "Hello Kevin, how are you? This is Vanessa."

"Vanessa, I know your voice anywhere is there something wrong? Let's see, you are calling to cancel tonight."

"See, there you go thinking the wrong thing. We are still on for tonight I just have to change the time that's all. I look forward to seeing you tonight."

"The same here Vanessa. I'm going into a meeting I will email you later with all the details."

"Okay Vanessa that's fine with me."

"Love You."

"I love you, as well Kevin."

Vanessa hangs up the phone.   She is sitting at her desk pondering on her life and her marriage. She says to herself, *I wasted twelve years of my life" with someone who I thought had my best interest at heart. I will never make that mistake again.*

It will take a lot for me to completely trust a man again… thanks again Tyrone Tyler.

CHAPTER THIRTEEN

Later that evening at the office of Shaunice Johnson Esq. Vanessa approaches the receptionist.

"Hi, I'm Zoie, how may I help you?"

"Good evening, my name is Vanessa Tyler I have an appointment with Ms. Johnson."

"Have a seat, I will let her know that you are here.

Ms. Johnson your sixty-thirty is here."

"Give her the paperwork and please tell her that I will be with her in about fifteen minutes."

"Okay Ms. Johnson, will do."

"Mrs. Tyler, can you please fill out his paperwork, Ms. Johnson will be with you in about fifteen minutes."

"Thank you so much."

"You are welcome."

Just as Vanessa finishes her paperwork, Ms. Johnson comes to greet her.

"Good evening, Mrs. Tyler, it's nice to finally meet you. Come with me."

"Before we get started can you, please do me a huge favor?"

Ms. Johnson is stunned, but she listens to Vanessa's request. "What is it?"

"Can you please call me Vanessa, and not Mrs. Tyler?"

"Is that all, of course I can do that?"

"Yes, that's all. Now I'm ready to answer any questions that you may have."

"Great, let's begin."

"How long were you and your husband married?"

"We were married for twelve and one half years."

"So why are you filing for divorce?"

"I'm filing for divorce because I found out that my husband of twelve and one half years has been cheating on me for five of those years."

"Is there any chance for a reconciliation with Tyrone?"

"There isn't a chance of reconciliation in this life time or the next one." Vanessa laughs as she says that.

"Vanessa are you absolutely sure?"

"I am positively sure. I took vows that said 'for better or for worse'. It didn't say for cheating and a baby."

"Excuse me, a baby?"

"Yes he has a mistress and a baby on the way. Now this changes everything."

"What does your husband do?"

"He just recently became a partner in his Brokerage Firm; he is the first black to achieve that status."

"Can you give me an estimate on what his salary is?"

"I want to say that he makes ten to twelve million a year and that's not with his commission."

"Hmmm. Is there property, cars, jewels?"

"We have three homes and four cars."

"It seems you have a wonderful life, Vanessa."

"I think you mean I *had* a wonderful life. It wasn't as wonderful as it seems. Yes I had homes, cars, clothes and jewels; but the one thing that was missing was that I couldn't give my husband any children, and that basically led him to cheat."

As Vanessa is thinking about her marriage, tears stream down her face.

Shaunice hands Vanessa a tissue and reassures her that everything is going to be okay. She tells Vanessa not to worry about anything. She has enough to file for divorce.

"Vanessa, just leave everything to me. The divorce proceedings shouldn't take too long if your husband doesn't contest it."

"Oh I am sure that he will try to contest it."

"He can try all he wants, but he has two things against him."

"What is that?"

"First of all, his attorney is going up against me. Secondly, I don't think that he wants anyone to know that he cheated on his wife for five years, especially now that he has made partner in his firm. He is going to keep this thing quiet as possible."

"That does make me feel a little more comfortable. I don't mean to cut you off, but I have an appointment at eight thirty with my husband's mistress."

"Vanessa as your attorney, I don't think that's a good idea. She might try and say that you are stalking her."

"We are meeting in a public place and I have two decoys that will be there as witnesses. Thank you for taking me on as a client this means a whole lot to me. So what's the next step?"

"Well tomorrow morning, I will take the papers to his attorney. His attorney will go over all the details of the divorce. I think what I asked for is fair, but we will see. "This could be easy, or your husband can try and drag this out as long as possible, which is a ploy. If your husband can get his attorney to drag this out, he figures you will get so discouraged that you will eventually throw in the towel and either drop the proceedings, or you will go back to him."

"One thing for sure, I don't care how long it takes, I will not go back to him. I'd rather be broke, happy and alone than to go back with him and be miserable. I really have to leave."

"Here's my card. Vanessa, call me in about a week. I should have heard something from your husband's attorney by then."

"Shaunice, you are so comforting, I will contact you in a week." Vanessa is rushing to get to her meeting with Kayla. As Vanessa gets closer to the restaurant she is having a change of heart, but she knows that she can't do that now because too many players are involved in this and she would look like a wimp.

Vanessa finally arrives at Chez Vous. She hopes Kayla doesn't act like a fool because she will slap the taste right out of her mouth.

Vanessa spots Kayla. She walks toward the table. "Hi Kayla, how are you doing?"

"Hi Vanessa, thank you so much for meeting with me. I guess you are wondering why I called you."

"Yes, I am wondering why you called me. I should be the last person you'd want to talk too."

"You are right about that but I wanted us to talk because I feel so bad about what happened with you and Tyrone and I wanted to tell you the real story. I wanted us to be able to talk and not scream at each other."

"Okay Kayla, how and where did you meet my husband?"

"I met Tyrone at a meeting he came over to me and introduced himself afterwards. He said that he was separated from you. He invited me out for drinks. I told him that I was not interested in dealing with a man who was with his wife. I didn't believe in breaking up anyone's home. Tyrone assured me that you two were not getting back together."

"Un-believable when did you finally figure out that Tyrone was still married?"

"I don't think you really want me to tell you that Vanessa you might be upset."

"No matter how upset I might get there is nothing I can do now, the damage has been done already."

"Tyrone took me to one of your homes. Correct me if I'm wrong, you have a home in New Jersey on Shirley Avenue. Well believe it or not we have a mutual friend, and Tyrone and I were leaving when our mutual friend asked what I was doing in your house. They said, 'I pray that his wife doesn't find out about the two of you'. I told them that Tyrone was separated from his wife, and they asked me, "Since when?' They told me that you guys had just celebrated your twelfth wedding anniversary with a big party. They actually showed me the proof. Vanessa; whether you believe it or not, I was totally stunned. I wanted to kill Tyrone right then and there; it took everything I had not to slap the taste out of his mouth. It was an embarrassing situation. We jumped in your car and I went off on him. He said that it was a marriage only on paper, but that he hadn't been in love with you for more than five years. I told him that he needed to tell you right away and he said that he would tell you that night when he got home. Well Vanessa, you know the rest."

Vanessa can't believe what she is hearing. She knows that Kayla isn't lying because they do have a house in New Jersey that's on Shirley Avenue and only a few people know that they a have a house in New Jersey. Vanessa wants to leap across the table and punch Kayla in her face, but she knows that she can't do that, so she keeps her calm.

"If you know that he lied to you why did you continue to see him? Didn't a red flag go off then or did you not care about him being married."

"Vanessa, now you know as well as I know that Tyrone is a very charming man and he can charm the panties off any woman if he can get the chance. So many times I told him to be honest and tell you what was going on, and I trusted and believed that he would tell you the truth. I threatened to tell you on many occasions, but Tyrone always managed to worm his way out of it. I even told him that he had one month to tell you, or I was spilling the beans and he went ballistic."

"That sounds just like Tyrone. Kayla I know this is going to sound strange, but I want to apologize to you because I was pissed that you would have an affair with a man who was married, but it's not totally your fault. What are you going to do about the baby? Tyrone is going to fight you tooth and nail on this."

"He can get visitation, but I don't think there is a judge in hell that will give him custody of my child. I have one more thing that I wanted to say to you. Vanessa, I am truly truly sorry. I didn't mean for this to happen, please forgive me."

"Kayla, beyond my better judgment, I do accept your apology. I have to go, but I just want to say I wish you all the best with the baby."

Vanessa leaves Chez Vous, she is feeling a little different about Kayla now.

Kevin and Vikki follow behind Vanessa a few minutes later. Each of them get into their cars and drive off. Vikki calls Vanessa while in her car." Hey Vikki, since I'm staying with you we can talk about my meeting with

Kayla when we get to the house."

They reach Vikki's house; of course Vikki is anxious to talk to Vanessa about what happened. Although Vanessa wants to talk to Vikki, she doesn't want to talk about the meeting with Kayla just yet, she has some other news that she wants to talk to Vikki about.

"Vikki, I want to talk to you."

"Girl, I know what happened at the restaurant."

"We will talk about that later, but I wanted to tell you about something else."

"What is it?"

"I know you said that I could stay with you for as long as I want, but I don't feel right so I am moving out at the end of the week."

"Vanessa you're what?"

"I'm moving."

"Wow, this is bittersweet."

"Yes Vikki it is bittersweet, but it had to happen and it's better to do it sooner than later."

"Vanessa, are you sure that you are going to be able to afford it?"

"Girl, now you know I was smart enough to save my money from the job. They paid me well and I got great bonuses. I never let on the amount of money I made. I didn't need to spend the money that I had because I always used Tyrone's credit card or I would take out what I needed for myself each week. I have enough for the next five years or more."

"So where are you moving to?"

"I'll be moving a few blocks from here. I found a nice four-bedroom house that I liked, so we will be neighbors."

"Girl that is great. We need to celebrate, I am happy for you. I want to see it."

"Well we can go there in a couple of days."

"Vanessa let's go tomorrow."

"Vikki, I wish that I could, but I have an appointment with Delicious; and when I'm finished getting my hair done, from there I am going to get some much needed rest. It has been a trying few days."

"Okay Vanessa, stop pretending. What happened at the meeting tonight with Kayla? You are being very quiet. You can talk to me."

"Well actually, the meeting went well. She wanted to apologize to me for the way that I found out about her and Tyrone. She also said that she had been telling Tyrone for years to tell me what was going on."

"I want to know why she dated him in the first place, she knew he was a married man."

"Not really, it seems that Tyrone told her that he and I were separated and that we were supposed to divorce."

"So let me ask you something Vanessa, when did Kayla find out that you guys were still married?"

"It seems that she went to the house in New Jersey and somehow she ended up meeting someone who knew both Tyrone and myself very well and they told her."

"So what are you going to do?"

"Nothing, she apologized to me for the pain that she and Tyrone caused at this point. I wish her and her baby all the best and I will pray for her. I know it's going to be hard for her to raise her baby by herself but she is a strong woman and I know that she will be able to handle it. Oh my goodness, that's Kevin. I don't want to talk to him right now. Vikki you can tell him anything I just need to get some rest right now."

"Hi Kevin, how are you doing?"

"Hey baby."

"I'm sorry Kevin, this is not Vanessa this is actually Vikki. Vanessa is asleep. That girl was so drained from all the drama from tonight that she just plopped down and fell asleep on the couch. Can I tell her that you called and have her call you sometime tomorrow?"

"That will be fine. Have a good evening."

"And you do the same."

"Vanessa that man likes you. How come you haven't slept with him yet?"

Because legally, I am still a married woman; but you can bet that as soon as my divorce is final, I'm going to let Kevin have his way with me." Both ladies share a nice laugh together. They both say good night to each other.

After a great night of rest Vanessa is getting dressed, eager to go to her job. Her phone is ringing; to her surprise, it is Tyrone. She doesn't want to be bothered with him, so she just lets the call go to her voice mail.

Tyrone leaves a message. "Hello Vanessa, this is your husband. I know you don't want to hear this right now, but I'm calling to check on you and to make sure that you are okay. I want to apologize to you for the way things turned out. I was wondering if we can get together and talk over dinner. I want to talk about a feasible settlement."

Vanessa is listening to the voice message that Tyrone has left on her phone. She is hesitant about returning his call because she knows that she will say something to him that she will regret later on. She calls her divorce attorney for legal advice.

"Vanessa, whatever you do, stay clear of Tyrone. You are not to have any contact with him, this will only help to bolster your case. Anything that he needs to say to you has to go through his attorney. As a matter of fact, I believe that I have his attorney's phone number. I will call him and order a cease and desist, which means the divorce proceedings can't be discussed by either party."

"That seems fair, thank you for clearing things up for me Shaunice. I must go now I have an appointment in approximately twenty minutes and I must not be late." Vanessa's appointment is actually with Delicious.

Vanessa jumps in her car, she will be at Desire's in no time for her appointment.

Shaniqua says to Delicious "Girl I'm tired. I partied last night."

"I know I can tell by your bags."

"What bags Delicious? I don't have any bags."

"Girl, yes you do, the bags under your eyes. Girl, you need to fix those things that's not cute."

"Shut up Delicious, my bags are not all that bad and I will take care of them after I get my coffee."

"Oh girl, please get me a cup also and tell them that you don't need any bags because you have two of them already." Delicious laughs.

"Delicious, it's too early in the morning for your nonsense; don't make me scratch your eyes out."

"Whatever, bring it on girl! I knew you were a bunch of hot air."

Vanessa and Vikki walk in.

Delicious says to Vanessa, "Hey darling, what is going on?"

"Nothing is going on. I'm doing as good as can be. Look I want you to cut it all off. I want something different and new."

"Okay, what's going on Vanessa? You want new and different and you want me to cut off all this niceness, girl what is it?"

"Delicious, I said I'm okay."

"Vanessa look, you can fool other people but you can never fool Delicious. I know when something is wrong, so what's going on girl?"

Vikki informs Delicious that something major happened in Vanessa's life over the past few days.

"Okay, it's time for girl talk, so do we need to close the shop down for a minute? Shut it down, I am listening."

"Vanessa came home and found Tyrone standing there in her living room with another woman."

"And did you cut his nuts off?"

"No I didn't cut his nuts off, it caught me off guard."

"And again I ask you Vanessa, did you cut his nuts off. Or at least try to cut them off."

"That's not the best part, this is the part that makes me really mad."

"Alright, spill it mighty mouth."

"Vanessa also found out that Tyrone's mistress is having a baby."

"You want to run that by me again, she is having a who?"

"I said Tyrone's mistress is having his baby."

"That's it. I'm done now. I'm mad now, go and get my gun. I'm gonna put some holes in his balls and I don't mean basketballs either."

Vikki tells the gang that the sad part in all of this is "that he has been having an affair with her for the past five years."

"Delicious wants to know who and where she is? I'm going to slice her every which way but loose."

"Her name is Kayla Jones."

"Oh hell to the no, Vanessa. I know you did not say that tramp is Tyrone's mistress. Umm hmm."

"Delicious, what's that about?"

Just as Delicious is about to say something there is a knock on the door, it's Kevin.

"Well look who we have here, Mr. Milk Chocolate, the kind that melts in your mouth and in your hands."

"Delicious will you stop it and let him in."

"Oh I will let him in alright."

Vikki tells Delicious, "Enough already."

"Hey everyone and Delicious."

"Kevin you don't have to be afraid of me I'll be gentle."

"No thank you Delicious.   I'm here to see Vanessa anyway."

"Good because she needs you now, more than ever."

"Vanessa baby, do you want to talk about it?"

"I'm really not in the mood to talk about it right now."

Kevin tells Vanessa that it is probably best to get it off her chest rather than holding it in.

"Look Kevin, I said that I don't want to talk about it right now. When I'm ready to discuss it with you I will tell you."

Vikki says to Vanessa,"Why are you talking to Kevin like that"? He is only asking you a question."

"Vikki, I said that I don't want to talk to him about it now, and I think that he should respect my wishes."

"Vikki it is okay. I thought Vanessa was different, but I guess that I was wrong. Well I think it is best that I leave. Good night everyone."

Delicious is shocked by the way Vanessa has treated Kevin. "Girl what in the world is wrong with you? That's a good man, I think you are confused. Kevin didn't cheat on you, Tyrone did; and Kevin is not the one you should be nasty with. Tyrone is the one you should be treating like that. You owe Kevin an apology."

"Vanessa I agree with Delicious on this one. Kevin has done nothing but been a good friend to you and to treat him the way you did was way out of line. You need to talk to him and don't wait too long to ask for his forgiveness."

Shaniqua chimes in on the conversation. "Vanessa I don't know a lot about relationships, but one thing I know for sure is that you are completely wrong. I haven't known you that long, but you seem like a nice person; this behavior seems so out of character for you."

"Okay will you all stop it! Actually I planned it that way. I have my reasons, there is a method to my madness. Everything is going to be alright between me and Kevin."

"If you say so Vanessa, now are you sure that you still want me to cut all of your hair off?"

"Delicious I am two hundred percent positive. I want it all gone. So get to cutting."

"If you say so Vanessa. I just don't want to cut your hair and then you look in the mirror and ask me why I didn't stop you from saying you want it off."

"Delicious if you aren't going to cut it then give me the scissors and I will do it myself, otherwise be quiet."

"That's my cue. I'm going to cut it off, no more questions asked. Okay now go under the dryer for ten minutes; after that I will blow your hair out and you can be on your merry way."

"Thank you Delicious."

"Delicious, I am really surprised at how she treated Kevin. I'm going to call him and apologize for her."

"Vikki you will do no such thing. She has to do that herself. Leave her love life alone, give it time. Those two will definitely work it out."

Vanessa is finished under the dryer and Delicious is about to style her when Kevin comes back to Desire's.

Everyone is shocked to see him.

Vanessa asks Kevin, "What in the world are you doing back here?"

"I want to know what's wrong with you. It's no need to hide it from me, so out with it now."

Vikki and Delicious are smiling. "Kevin it's not that I don't want to tell you I just don't know if now is the right time."

"Well anytime that something concerns you, then it's the right time."

"Okay Kevin, since you won't give up, here it is. After twelve years of marriage, I caught my husband with another woman and she's having his baby. They have been seeing each other over the past five years."

"I love it this is the best news I heard all day."

Vikki is shocked by what Kevin just said. "Kevin what do you mean you're loving this, can't you see that my girl is hurt?"

"Vikki you don't get it do you? I have been in love with this woman since the first day I laid eyes on her. I knew she was a good woman and I knew that there was something missing in my life. I held my peace, but each night that we were apart I prayed and asked GOD to release her from that relationship and bring her into my life; and he did, he gave me My True Love."

"Kevin that's nice. I want to thank you for sticking in there with me."

"Woman I'm yours… and I'm here to stay."

"Hey guys, please let me finish what I wanted to say earlier. I knew that Tyrone was messing with that tramp Kayla, I knew it when I ran into them at the hair convention. Tyrone was shocked to see me, I never saw a black man turn so red. I'm just glad it's out in the open now, Vanessa, now you see what he isn't about and what kind of creep that he really is. He was going to play this out as long as he could. You know, Jesus knew what he was doing; he got tired of covering for Tyrone so he had to expose him. Vanessa I am so sorry."

"Delicious what do you have to be sorry about?"

"Because Kayla became a client of mine, but she will be gone as of today."

"You don't have to let her go as a client. I know you are going to think that I have lost my mind, but Kayla and I actually had a meeting last night."

"Vanessa what in the world could that woman have possibly wanted with you? I hope you gave it to her good."

"Actually Delicious, I didn't do anything to her. We actually had a very civil conversation. Believe it or not, she apologized to me for the way that things ended between me and Tyrone. She said that she has been telling him for years to be truthful to me and he wasn't. I believe her and I accepted her apology. Look, we aren't friends or anything like that. I am now and will always be the better woman. I'm praying for her and for her baby. It's not easy being a single mom, raising a child on your own."

"Sweetie, I think it's best for all parties, especially her, that I cut her loose as a client because I might cut more than her hair off. Vanessa, you are a wonderful person thinking of me when you are going through so much drama; but I don't think I will feel good knowing what she and Tyrone did to one of my closest friends."

Delicious wants to know if Kayla and Tyrone are officially a couple now.

"Truth be told guys I'm not sure what's going on between her and Tyrone, and I really don't care. All I want is for my divorce to be final so that I can move on with my life and pray that God blesses me with a good man and that he will not be a cheater."

Kevin tells Vanessa that God already blessed her with him.

Vikki and Delicious both suggest that Vanessa go and have you some fun and go and work it with Kevin.

Vanessa emphatically says "I'm still a married woman."

Vikki raises her voice a little to her friend and says "Vanessa, at this point in your life who cares what you do, you are in the process of a divorce."

"I understand what you are all saying, but you guys know that Tyrone knows everyone; and all I need is for one of his friends to see me with another man and that will be all the ammunition Tyrone will need to prolong the divorce. So, as much as I would like to, I can't work anything with anyone right now."

Vanessa tells Delicious, "If you learn how to work it maybe you can get some too."

"Vanessa don't get it twisted. I can drop it, work it and catch it all at the same time. They don't call me Delicious for nothing." Everyone laughs.

"Well that's my cue, this time I am leaving for real. Vanessa I love you and I will call you tomorrow for a lunch date."

"Okay Kevin, we will talk tomorrow."

"Come on Vanessa, I have got to get home. I haven't seen Antonio in a couple of days, and I want to spend some time with him."

"Vanessa, I forgot to ask you where are you staying?"

"Delicious, I was staying with Vikki; but as of today I am no longer at her place."

"Do you need a place to stay because I have an extra bedroom?"

"Thanks, but no thanks, Delicious. I have a place. I am renting a house until the divorce proceedings are over."

"Alright now, but if you need anything, please don't hesitate to call me. I will help you any way that I can."

"Thanks guys, it's really good to know that I can count on you all when I'm in need. You all are such good friends, I love all of you. Now let's go."

Delicious wants to lock up the shop and go home. "Ladies, it has been a very long and trying day."

"Delicious, you are so right. "

"Vanessa, make sure you call me tomorrow to schedule your next appointment."

"Hold on guys, it's my sweetie. Hi Antonio."

"Hey baby where are you? I'm at home waiting for you."

"I am on my way I was at getting my hair done I will be home soon."

"Vikki, Antonio is sweet on you. So when is that Caramel Coated man coming back to Desire's?"

"Never Delicious, you scared him away; he is permanently scarred for life."

"I have a man at home I cannot stand here and continue to talk to any of you. I love you Delicious and I love you Vanessa, but I'm leaving."

Delicious walks Vanessa to her car.

"Thank you so much Delicious, you are so nice. In all the years that I have known you, I never asked you this but I'm going to ask you now. Why don't you use your given name Lavell? I think it is such a nice name, it's different."

Vanessa I can't really answer that, people have been calling me Delicious since I was little. See I had fat cheeks and my mother and grandmother would say that my cheeks were so fat and cute that they were delicious enough to bite and Delicious just stuck. I do use Lavell for business purposes, so does that answer your question?"

"It sure does, now go home. Bye sweetie."

"Good bye Lavell."

As Vanessa is driving home she realizes that she has to get her clothes from her house. She hasn't seen Tyrone in days and she really doesn't want to go near there, but she has too. She decides that she will go to her house in the morning after Tyrone has left for work, this way she won't have to run into him and she can get what she needs. Vanessa arrives home safely she calls the gang to let them all know she has made it in. She calls Kevin before she turns in for the evening. "Hi Kevin, this is Vanessa."

"Vanessa, you do that every time you call, I know your voice. Baby I know your voice anywhere."

"Well I'm about to turn in for the evening, but I wanted to let you know that I made it home safely and I look forward to seeing you tomorrow."

"Okay baby, I'm going to turn in as well. I was waiting for you to get home before I went to sleep, and now that I know you have arrived safely I can fall asleep. See you tomorrow. I just threw you a kiss Vanessa."

"That's what that was Kevin? I caught it." Vanessa is smiling.

"Vanessa until we talk tomorrow, be safe."

It's a nice warm and sunny Friday morning. Vanessa is up staring out the window of her new home, still in a daze over the crumbling of her marriage. She knows that she has to go to her other house, but it's going to be strange to go there and not be able to sleep in her bed again. She can't believe that she has to start from scratch. *Maybe this is a blessing in disguise, or maybe God wanted to show me that I could do better. I can't dwell on this now. I have to muster up the strength to go there and get my things.*

Vanessa gets in her car and drives thirty five minutes to her former place. She is relieved to see that Tyrone has already left for work, now she can get what she needs. She gets out of the car and heads to the house, she prays that Tyrone hasn't changed the locks. Vanessa is relieved that he didn't, she puts the key in the door and proceeds to go inside. She goes upstairs to get some things out of the closet. She is walking down the stairs as she reaches the bottom stair Tyrone appears out of nowhere; it seems that once again he forgot something and he had to double back.

"Vanessa what are you doing here?"

"I just stopped by to get some of my clothes, that is all. I'm leaving."

"Vanessa wait, how are you? Are you okay? I called you the other night. Did you get my message?"

"Yes I got your message, Tyrone. I was surprised to hear from you."

"Why would you be surprised to hear from me Vanessa? Whether you believe it or not, I still do care for you."

"Did you care for me when you were cheating on me with Kayla? Tyrone I gave you the best years of my life. I supported you in every endeavor. You could have at least been up front with me and just said how you really felt about me."

"Vanessa, I loved you from the day I met you and I never wanted anyone else but you. You know how much I wanted kids, but you acted as though you were too busy to make a family."

"Tyrone don't you dare turn this around on me. I wanted a family just as much as you did, but you made me feel that I was less of a woman, you made me feel as though you were ashamed to touch me for some reason. Many nights I cried myself to sleep because of the way you treated me. Why did you lie to me all those times? Why didn't you just man up and say that you found someone else to love?"

"Vanessa I really don't know why, I guess I was scared and nervous at the same time."

"Tyrone what were you scared of?"

"I was scared that you would not be able to handle me having an affair and you would have a nervous breakdown."

"Wow, thanks for thinking so highly of me. Tyrone, I am stronger than you think. You know what? I have got to go, truth is that I can't stand to look at you. You are definitely not the man that I married."

"Vanessa just go, and I hope that you have all of your things."

"Tyrone, now you know that I can't possibly get all my things at one time. I will have to come back another day to get them."

"Please call before you come so I can set up a time for you to get the rest of your things."

"The nerve of you. I will come back when I get a chance."

"No you will not; you have to arrange a time to get your things. I need to be here when you come back".

"Tyrone you are a bastard."

"Vanessa, how dare you call me names. That's why we aren't together now."

"You have a lot of nerve Tyrone. You aren't a bastard, you are a coward bastard. You did this not me."

"Get the hell out of my house. I am going to make this divorce a living hell for you."

"Really! That's what you think. You cheated I didn't. You are making your own life a living hell."

"Vanessa, we will see if you get anything from me."

"Tyrone we will see about that. Look I really don't have time for this, I have to take these things home and then get ready for work."

"Like I said before, call before you come if you want to get your things. I will have them boxed up for you."

"Picture that, Tyrone. I'm still your wife, the divorce isn't final yet."

"Picture it, Vanessa. Step in this house without calling before you come over and you will see what will happen."

"Tyrone, please do not go there with the threats."

"Leave, Vanessa."

"I'll be more than happy to get out of here."

"Good bye Creep."

"Good bye Vanessa." He slams the door behind her. Tyrone is heartbroken about him and Vanessa, or so he pretends to be. Of course he calls Kayla thinking that she will be at his beck and call.

"Hello Kayla, this is Tyrone. I was calling to see how you and our baby are doing?"

"Hello Tyrone how are you doing? Me and my baby are fine."

"Kayla, why are you playing games with me?"

"What in the world are you talking about Tyrone?"

"You know what I'm talking about Kayla, our baby. I'm tired of you thinking that you are the only one that is the parent of our baby."

"As far as I am concerned Tyrone, you and I are not going to be in a relationship."

Kayla, if you don't want to be in a relationship with me that's fine, but you can't stop me from raising my child."

"Tyrone you can be in your child's life. I will allow you to have visitation rights, but that's as far as it goes."

"Kayla, we will see about that."

"Try and stop me Tyrone."

"Kayla, this is a fight that you cannot and will not win."

"I will let you think that Tyrone. I have had enough of your mouth. Get off my phone, you and I have nothing to say."

Tyrone hears a dial tone on the other end.

Kayla has got to be crazy if she thinks that all I will have is visitation rights with my child. She has another thing coming to her. She doesn't know who she is dealing with at all.

Kayla is thinking out loud. *That Negro has lost his mind. I have a trick for him. I will take him to court and ban him from having any rights to my baby. Who in the hell does he think he is talking too? This is war. Lord knows this has got to be Michael's baby. I will die if this isn't his baby, this will definitely break Michael's heart.*

Kayla gets up to call Michael but she has a dizzy spell and has to sit back in her chair. The phone conversation with Tyrone has upset her dearly. She doesn't want to alarm Michael because he likes to go overboard. Kayla decides that she will keep this to herself. She will just sit down for a few moments to calm her nerves. Kayla has to act fast because she knows that Tyrone can be cruel and sneaky. She musters up enough strength, however, to call an attorney to see what rights she has. Just as she says this Tyrone calls.

Tyrone has a lot of nerve calling me after the way he talked to me.

"Kayla, please pick up the phone."

Kayla decides to answer the phone, after Tyrone has called three times. If she doesn't he will keep calling. "Yes Tyrone, what is it and why are you calling me?"

"I know you don't want to talk to me right now, but I wanted to call and apologize for my actions. I want us to get along for the sake of the baby."

"Tyrone, beyond my better judgment I guess you're right."

"And Kayla, who knows, maybe you will change your mind about the two of us and we can be together like you always wanted."

"Like I always wanted Tyrone, so you aren't interested in being in a relationship with me?"

"Kayla, you know that I was and I am still in love with you and want to be with you. But of course, it's not the right time."

"So when is the right time, Tyrone?"

"As soon as my divorce is over, then the three of us can be a family."

"The three of us? You and I are only two people."

"Kayla, what about the baby? That makes three of us."

"Oh, I guess you're right. Well I need to go, Tyrone. I accept your apology and thank you for calling. We will speak again soon."

"Okay, thank you Kayla. I appreciate that and I feel so much better now. I want us to be on good terms."

"Take care, Tyrone."

"Take care."

Kayla laughs after she hangs up with Tyrone. She does not want to be in a relationship now, or in the future. Her heart and soul are with Michael. She can't wait for them to get married and to have this baby.

CHAPTER FOURTEEN

It's Saturday afternoon. Antonio has called Vanessa and asked her to meet him at Vale's Jewelers at twelve thirty. He wants to pick out the perfect ring for Vikki.

"Hello Antonio, I would love to go with you to Vale's. I'm so excited for you and Vikki, she is going to pass out when you propose to her. Okay now, how do you plan on proposing to her? You have to do something different."

"I will call you back with a few ideas and you can let me know which one of them you like."

"Okay Vanessa, that sounds okay. I am happy and nervous, all at the same time."

"You will be okay Antonio, you are getting a great woman."

"You haven't told me anything that I don't already know. Thanks for helping me and I will see you at three."

"See you then Antonio."

Vanessa has to find the perfect way for Antonio to propose to Vikki. She comes up with a great idea but she doesn't know if Antonio will like the idea, she calls him back. "Antonio, I have a brilliant idea but I don't know if you are going to like it."

"Lay it on me, Vanessa."

"Well here it is. Since you have to renew your contract why don't we draw up a contract and you can ask her to read it and ask her what she thinks of the contract and as she reads it the contract will say *Will You Marry Me Vikki?* So what do you think Antonio?"

"Vanessa, that is brilliant."

"Since I work for a law firm and I deal with contracts, I will type it for you and make sure you have it with you before you guys go to dinner tonight. How does that sound?"

"That sounds perfect Vanessa."

"Antonio, let me go so I can type the contract now and I will have everything in place for you tonight. Where are you going for dinner?"

"I haven't thought about that Vanessa, do you have any ideas?"

"I have the perfect place Antonio, you can use my house. I think it's perfect for you to propose to Vikki. I will call in a few favors. How does seven o'clock work for you?"

"That is a perfect time, it gives me time to get the ring, run home, change clothes and get to your place."

"Okay Antonio, you are on."

As soon as Vanessa hangs up the phone with Antonio she calls her friend Terence. He is a famous r &b singer. He is great friends with her and he happens to be home.

"Hello may I speak to Terence, please."

"This is his mother Miss Pauline, may I ask who's calling for Terence?"

"Hi Ms. Pauline, how are you? This is Vanessa, it's been a while since we have spoken."

"Vanessa, the name sounds familiar?"

"Vanessa Tyler."

"I'm sorry I don't know a Vanessa Tyler."

"Miss Pauline, you know me by my maiden name Jackson."

"Oh my goodness Vanessa Jackson, little Vanessa Jackson from Oak Grove Street."

"Yes Miss Pauline, that's me."

"Child it's good to hear from you. Sorry about not remembering your married name. I'm used to Jackson, next time please say that name. Do you need to talk to Terence? He is going to be so surprised when I tell him you're on the phone."

"Miss Pauline, please do not tell him I'm on the phone. I want to see if he will be able to figure it out for himself."

"Terence, there is someone on the phone who would like to speak to you."

"Who is it mom?"

"Boy come here and find out."

"Mom!"

"Don't mom me boy, come and get the phone."

"Okay, I'm coming."

"Here he is. It was nice speaking with you."

"Same here, Miss Pauline I will come and stop by soon."

"Please do that I would love to see you, it's been too long."

"It sure has."

"Hello, this is Terence."

"Hi Terence, how are you?"

Hesitating to say anything else, he is trying to figure out who the caller is. "I'm great now who is this?"

"Terence, I'm hurt that you don't recognize my voice, as long as we have been friends."

"I have a lot of friends."

"It's Vanessa, how are you Terence?"

"Vanessa who?"

"Terence, you really don't know who it is? It's Vanessa."

"I know a couple of Vanessas."

"Listen, I don't have time for games."

"Okay Terence, it's Vanne."

"Vanne?"

"Yes, now how many women do you call Vanne?"

"Oh my goodness, where have you been? How are you?"

"I can't believe that I'm talking to you, it's been so long since we have spoken."

"I know. Are you busy? But I really need to speak to you."

"No, I'm not busy at all."

"Can I stop by? I need to talk to you."

"Sure you can."

"Alright I will be there in about 20 minutes. See you then."

Vanessa arrives at Terence's house.

He is so excited to see his friend. He opens the door and just stares at her. He can't believe how beautiful Vanessa is.

"My goodness Vanne, you are more beautiful than I imagined. Girl get in here now, mom Vanne is here."

"Hi Miss Pauline, you look wonderful."

"Vanessa you look awesome. I'm sorry about interrogating you on the phone earlier, but Terence has so many people calling him for money that I have to intercept the calls."

"It is quite understandable, Miss Pauline."

"So what brings you here, may I ask?"

"Well I need a favor from Terence."

"And before you say anything, please listen. I am not asking for money. Well Terence, I don't know if you remember Vikki Black."

"Yes I remember her, did something happen to her?"

"No it's nothing like that. She has been dating a guy named Antonio Anderson."

"Why does that name sound so familiar?"

"He is only the best running back in the game. Well he wants to propose to Vikki tonight and I was wondering if you would sing something special for them. I know that it's short notice."

"Normally I would say no, but for you Vanessa... I mean Vanne... I will be more than happy to help out."

"Great! I'm preparing a dinner for them at my new house."

"Your new house? Yes my new house."

"How are things with you and Tyrone? That was such a beautiful wedding. I can't believe you guys have been married for twelve years, it seems like yesterday."

"Well Miss Pauline, I would rather you and Terence hear it from me than to hear it from someone else. Tyrone and I are in the process of a divorce."

"What! Vanessa you have to be kidding me. I never would have thought you two would be getting a divorce, you guys seemed like the perfect couple. You two were perfect for each other."

"I thought the same thing. Tyrone cheated on me, he has been having an affair for the past five years with an attorney and she is going to have his baby."

"Vanessa, I am so sorry. Tyrone cheating on you and having a baby with another woman; that is not cool at all."

"Ms. Pauline, it's been hard, but I will get through this. But this is not about me."

"You are a good friend, Vanne to do this for Vikki. I will be at your place at six thirty."

"It's funny that you said that time because I was going to ask you to be there at six thirty. The dinner is at seven o'clock. Well I need to go. I have to call in another favor to prepare a nice dinner for two. Terence it was good seeing you again."

"And Miss Pauline, now that I am in the area I will stop by more often."

"Thank you Vanne, that's good because I'm always on the road and I worry about her."

"You don't have to worry about her anymore.   I live about twenty minutes from here. See you guys later."

Vanessa rushes to get to the caterers to see if they are able to come to her home by six o'clock. She is running late for her twelve-thirty appointment with Antonio. She calls him to let him know that she will be there soon.

Antonio tells her that it's okay because he is stuck in traffic.

"That's perfect, now I don't feel so bad. If I get to the jewelers before you do I will look at the rings and pick the ring that I think Vikki would like."

"Thanks Vanessa, you are a great help."

"I hope this doesn't take too long I have to get home to set up. And I am having furniture that is being delivered at three thirty this afternoon."

"It won't be too long Vanessa, I am almost there."

"Okay, see you soon. I will call Vikki. I have to find a way to get her to my house." Vanessa calls Vikki. "Hey girl how are you?"

"Vanessa, I'm doing okay."

"What are you doing tonight about seven-thirty?"

"Nothing at all, I would love to get together. I think it would be nice for you to get out, especially since you are going through a tough time right now Vanessa."

"Good I want to invite you to dinner at my new place. You need to come dressed cute."

"Why do I need to come dressed cute to see your new place."

"Because I asked you to, that's why. It's a new beginning for me and it's my way of saying thank you for always having my back."

"Since you put it that way, I will be there."

"Thanks let me go, I am having my furniture delivered in a few hours and I need to get home."

"Where are you?"

"Shopping where else?"

"You mean to tell me, Vanessa that you didn't ask me if I wanted to go?"

"It was a spur of the moment thing, otherwise I definitely would have contacted you."

"I will let it go this time, don't do it again."

"Vikki you are too funny. I am sorry, I promise to never leave you out of my shopping sprees. I am also meeting a friend and he just came."

"Girl are you meeting up with Kevin?"

"No I am not, I am meeting another friend."

"You go girl, you must tell me about him. I think Tyrone cheating was the best thing that happened to you, now you are getting to meet some eligible candidates."

"It's not like that at all. I have to go, my friend just pulled up and they are standing in front of me and it's rude to be on the phone with you. Vikki I will see you at seven thirty. I will text you my address in a little while."

"Okay girl, see you in a few hours. Love You."

"Hey there Antonio. I picked out a ring that I know Vikki would like."

"Vanessa that is so beautiful, that's the ring. Damn,I'm a man and I love it."

"Antonio you need to stop it, don't you want to pick out anything else."

"Vanessa trust me, this is the one. Let me ask you would you pick this right? I might think it's a bit much for me, but it is gorgeous, Vikki is going to love it. You must really love her."

"I do love her, why do you say that?"

"Because you are spending fifteen thousand dollars on this ring."

"Vanessa, you can't put a price on love and I want to spend my life with this woman."

Tears begin to stream down Vanessa's face, this is bringing back memories of her marriage to Tyrone.

"Vanessa, my bad. I didn't mean to remind you of what's going on in your relationship. You are a strong woman to stand here and pick out engagement rings. If I were a woman, I would be too devastated to look at rings."

"Vikki is my best friend and she has a great man in her life and I believe that you will treat her the way she deserves to be treated. I am happy that she has finally found someone special in her life."

"She is the love of my life. I knew that she wanted me for me and not for what I do. She is different, not like any of the other women that I have met. That's why I knew I had to make this official. I had to make her my life partner. I could not see myself with anyone else."

"Antonio I don't mean to cut you off, but I have got to get out of here. I need to meet the delivery guys in about an hour. See you at seven o'clock."

"See you then."

Vanessa races like a bat out of hell to get to her house before the delivery guys get there. She does everything in her power not to get stopped by the police. She made it home without incident, just in the nick of time.

The time is drawing near for what will be the event of the night. Everything was falling into place. How happy Vanessa was for her best friend getting engaged to the man of her dreams.

Everyone arrives on time and everything looks great. Antonio is nervous. As Vikki arrives at Vanessa's home she notices Antonio's car in Vanessa's driveway. She wonders why he would be at her best friend's house. She is furious. She rings the bell and is ready to curse both of them out. She walks in the house, but she is feeling a bit uncomfortable because she doesn't know what to expect. Now she has a man who is cheating on her.

"Hello, is there anyone here?"

"Yes Vikki darling, I'm in the dining room."

"Antonio, I don't know where the dining room is, this is my first time here. It's my first time also it's down the hall to the right."

Vanessa comes down stairs, nicely dressed.

Now Vikki is really bothered.

"Vikki why are you standing in the hallway why didn't you go to the dining room? Antonio is waiting for you he has something for you."

"Vanessa, why are you dressed like that and why is my boyfriend in your house?"

"Vikki, will you just go to the dining room you will find out."

"Vanessa, are you and Antonio seeing each other?"

"Vikki, I am upset that you would think such a thing about me. I am your friend and I would never do anything to violate that."

Antonio yells from the dining room to Vikki demanding that she gets to the dining room now!

Vikki is not happy about this, but she is going to the dining room not knowing what to expect. When she walks to the dining room, she is shocked by what she sees. Oh my goodness, this is unbelievable.

"I hope you like it baby."

"Antonio I love it. What is going on here?"

"I need you to sit down."

"This place looks gorgeous."

"Well thank Vanessa because she did all the work."

"Nice job Vanessa, but I still don't know what's going on. Would someone please let me in on this?"

"Have a seat and welcome to Chez Vanessa."

"This is wonderful.   I love this and I love you Antonio."

"I love you more. Vikki, you and I have been together for the past nine months. I have never felt like this about any woman, until I met you. I can't see my life without you. So I wanted to have this dinner for you. And I have a special gift for you, but I will give you that later."

"Vikki, I have a surprise for you and Antonio. I asked a friend to come and help me with this dinner and he was willing. Guys this is for the both of you, hope you enjoy." Both of them are stunned when they see the number one r and b singer, Terence, standing in Vanessa's dining room serenading both of them.

"Vanessa how in the world did you get Terence to come here and sing for us?"

"Terence is an old friend of mine. He was home this week and I asked him for a favor and he said that he would be more than happy to sing for you guys."

"Vikki is brought to tears."

Vanessa sees how romantic this is, she steps away and calls Kevin.

"Hey baby how are you?"

"I'm great, are you busy tonight?"

"No I'm not, what's up?"

"I would like to invite you to see my new place."

"I will be there with bells on. I should be there in about thirty minutes. Send me your address when you have a moment. I look forward to seeing you."

"Same here, Kevin and I'm sending it to you as we speak."

Vanessa comes back to the dining room. "Listen you two I will be your waitress. I hope you enjoy your meal."

"Vanessa this looks fantastic. You have all my favorite foods here."

"I hope you both like it."

"I am sure that we will."

"Well, I am going to let you two eat and have a nice quiet dinner. I will be back in about twenty minutes." As Vanessa says that her doorbell rings; it's Kevin.

"Kevin, you made it. I am glad. I was so lonely."

"Well you don't have to be lonely anymore. I am here for you. Wait a minute, where is my sugar. Here you are. Hold up, what's with the peck on the cheek woman! I want a real kiss."

"Kevin, that will have to wait."

"Vanessa why do I have to wait? You didn't call me to come over here to tell me to wait."

"Kevin, there are other people here that's why you have to wait."

"Why didn't you say so, now who is in the house?"

"Antonio and Vikki are in the dining room eating dinner."

"Then let's go join them."

"Wait, not yet. I am trying to give them some privacy. Antonio is going to propose to Vikki and I am waiting until that time comes, then we can go and be witnesses as he proposes to her."

"Oh I understand, but that doesn't mean that we can't enjoy each other's company."

"Kevin I really don't want to do anything until we are alone. It's not a good time right now. Let's go see what the lovebirds are doing?"

"Hey guys how was your dinner?"

"Everything was fine, Vanessa."

"Terence, you are still here. I thought you would have been gone by now."

"I decided that since this is a special occasion, I have one more song to dedicate to Antonio and Vikki."

"Kevin is in awe, oh shoot Vanessa. Terence is standing in your dining room. How did you get him to come to your house and sing for them?"

"Let me introduce you before he sings another song. Kevin this Terence, Terence this is Kevin. Can I put my bid in now, can you sing at my wedding?"

"Sure man, just let me know the time, date and place. You can give all of your information to Vanessa."

"Vanessa didn't tell you? She is going to be my future wife."

"She is?"

"I haven't officially mentioned it to her yet, but as soon as her divorce is over I will make it official."

"Okay you guys, are you ready for dessert?"

"Yes we are."

"Okay, is it alright if Kevin and I join the two of you?"

"We don't have a problem with it at all. The more the merrier. Vanessa, I need you two to sit at the table. Vikki I need you to come here."

"Earlier I said that I wanted to spend the rest of my life with you, and I still mean that. With that being said I have this contract that I want you to read, it's a contract extension and I want to get your input on it."

The contract is actually a marriage proposal, it reads you are the only woman for me and I would be honored if you would be the future Mrs. Anderson. "Vikki Black will you marry me?"

Vikki gladly yells out "Yes! I will marry you, Antonio. You are the only man I want to spend the rest of my days with."

Antonio places the six carat round white gold ring on Vikki's finger.

"Antonio this is perfect I love this ring, how did you know that this was the ring that I liked?"

"I had help. Vanessa has been amazing through this whole process. I told her about this yesterday, and she worked her magic."

"That's why she is my best friend. Vanessa thank you so much for doing this for me and Antonio, this is a night that I will never ever forget. You have helped make my dreams a reality."

"Kevin, thank you for coming. I hope and pray that one day Vikki and I will be able to help you to celebrate your engagement."

"Okay you guys can go to the living room while I clean up in here."

"Vanessa, let me help you."

"Kevin, thank you, but I can do it."

"Look Kevin, if Vanessa says go into the living room, then we need to go and do what she says. The game is on."

"Vanessa, I'm coming to help."

"No you will not Vikki, you just got engaged. Spend it with your new fiancée."

"Vanessa, I said I'm going to help you out and I want to help out, there are no if's ands or butts about it. Move over girl. There is no way I am going to let you go through all of this for me and Antonio and not help you. I'll tell you what, I will wash and you can dry."

"How about this Vikki I will wash and you can dry, I don't want anything to happen to that gorgeous ring."

"I hear you, Vanessa. I could cry right now."

"Vikki girl, what's wrong? You should be happy."

"That's why I could cry, I am so happy at this moment. I never in a million years thought that I would meet such a wonderful man as Antonio. You know that when it comes to being in a relationship, I didn't have much luck. Well the Bible is right. It says he that findeth a wife findeth a good thing. I know that I am a good woman and I'm not being conceited about it."

"Vikki, you're not being conceited. Forgive me, now I'm crying. I feel so stupid right now."

"Vanessa, why are you crying?"

"Because my best friend is getting married and I'm in the process of a divorce. I thought that you would be coming to me for advice on your marriage. Look how things turn out. You are going to be a beautiful bride and a wonderful wife."

"I have a question to ask you, Vanessa."

"Sure, I am listening."

"Vanessa, would you please be my maid of honor?"

"Of course I would, just let me know when the date is. Girl let me see this ring again. This is so beautiful we have good taste."

"Girl we definitely do." Both girls laugh. As they finish cleaning, they move to the living room with the men. They are both comforted in knowing that they are with men who love them both.

It is nine thirty in the evening, everyone has to get up for work. Terence is about to leave when both Antonio and Vikki thank him for the personal serenade. He tells them both that they are welcome.

Antonio and Vikki have to leave, Vikki is still basking in her engagement with the man of her dreams. She can't wait to show off her ring. Antonio hasn't stopped blushing since Vikki said yes, now he can sign his contract extension.

Vanessa invites Kevin to stay with her; she doesn't want to be alone tonight. It's time that she gives this relationship a chance. She cannot worry about Tyrone anymore, she gave him the best twelve years of her life. Now it's time for her to move on; but she still has to be sensible, she isn't divorced from Tyrone just yet.

Kevin is excited about Vanessa's invitation to spend the night.

But she wants to be crystal clear that she is still legally married to Tyrone and that she is not going to sleep with Kevin, until her divorce becomes final. She hopes that Kevin will understand and if he doesn't, then maybe he isn't the man for her.

Kevin makes it known to Vanessa that he understands; he doesn't agree with it, but he understands what she is saying.

All she wants from Kevin right now is to be held in his arms.

He obliges to her wishes.

Vanessa falls asleep in his arms. This is the best sleep that she has had since she found out that Tyrone cheated on her. More than anything she wants the divorce proceedings to be over soon. She prays that Tyrone doesn't contest it, so that they both can move forward with their lives. She needs to go to her house to get the rest of her things before she goes to work.

It's a sunny Monday morning. You can smell freshness in the air, the birds are chirping. What a beautiful summer day.

"Morning, sleepy head how did you sleep last night?"

"Holding you in my arms, Vanessa made this night special. It was the best sleep I had in a long time, it felt weird but good. You are the first woman that I have wanted to be with since my wife died. No one else has made me feel that way."

"Aw Kevin that was such a nice thing to say and I have never felt this way about another man before. I look forward to spending more time with you."

"That goes double for me Vanessa. Sorry I have to run, but I have an early meeting I'll call you later."

"Okay Kevin, that's fine."

"Wait a minute, where's my sugar?"

"Are you trying to be fresh so early in the morning?"

"Yes, I am. They both share a laugh."

"Go before I change my mind and give you a pre divorce sample."

"That would be fine with me, Vanessa."

"I bet it would, now leave. Vanessa is smiling as she says this."

She is about to do something that most people would think is crazy, but she is going to call Tyrone, not because she wants to reconcile or anything. She just wants to know when he is leaving so she can come and get her things out of the house. She has to find a way to be clever about this. She begins to dial Tyrone.

"Good morning Tyrone this is Vanessa how are you doing this morning?"

"Vanessa I am great, what's on your mind?"

"There is nothing on my mind I was calling to see how you are doing and to make sure everything is okay with you. Even though are marriage ended, it doesn't mean that we can't be cordial to one another. Did you forget that we have known each other for sixteen years and we have been married for twelve of those sixteen years? You don't just throw that away."

"Vanessa you are right. I never stopped loving you, and I would love for us to be friends. Well it was good speaking to you. I have to get ready for work now, I have a busy day."

"Likewise, and I have a busy day, as well. Have a wonderful day Tyrone."

"Thank you."

Great that means I can go and get my things. And the Oscar for best actress goes to Vanessa Tyler. Vanessa laughs, as she prepares to get dressed. She calls Vikki and Antonio to see if they are willing to help her get her things out of the house.

"Vikki, it's me Vanessa. I know that you are still basking in your engagement, but I need your help."

"What is it girl?"

"I just called Tyrone…" Before Vanessa can get another word out of her mouth Vikki is going off on her.

"Are you crazy why did you call him? You need to stay as far away from him as possible, until your divorce is final."

"Vikki take a breather. I only called Tyrone to find out if he would be home because I want to get the rest of my things."

"Okay then, what did he say?"

"Nothing I pretended that I wanted to be friends with him and that I was checking on him. Girl, you know that I really don't care what Tyrone does with his life, as long as he doesn't prolong the divorce proceedings, everything will be okay with me. So are you going to help me out, or what?"

"Girl you know I have your back."

"I knew I could count on you. I will pick you up in an hour is that okay?"

"That's great, it will give me time to get ready."

"Thanks girl, I knew I could count on you."

"Vanessa, do we need any reinforcement?"

"Yes we do, who can we get? I got the perfect person in mind."

"Vanessa, you do?"

"Yes I do. Delicious would be perfect."

"You are right. I never would have thought of him. Call him and see what he says."

Vanessa calls Delicious. "Hey there Delicious this is Vanessa."

"Hey sista, what can I do for you this morning?"

"I need your help."

"What do you need my help with?"

"I need to get the rest of my things out of my house and I want to do it when Tyrone leaves. He should be leaving for work in about forty five minutes."

"Oh I am definitely there. Okay, it is nine thirty now. Let's meet at your house at ten thirty is that okay?"

"That is perfect, it will give me time to stop and get Vikki see you soon."

"Gotcha, see you in an hour and be on time. I have a twelve o'clock appointment. I don't like to keep my people waiting."

"We should be finished way before then."

All three arrive at Tyrone's residence prepared to get all of Vanessa's belongings.

To Vanessa's surprise, most of her things are already boxed up. The nerve of Tyrone, he thinks that he is so slick.

Vikki responds to Vanessa and asks her why she is so upset. "What did Tyrone do now? Doesn't it make it easier for you to get your things?"

"No it doesn't if one box is out of place Tyrone will know that I was here, so now I can only get the few things that are left in my closet and drawers."

"Then let's get them Vanessa, I have an appointment coming at twelve noon and I know that you and Vikki need to get to work as soon as possible. You will just have to come back at another time. We are trespassing, so please hurry up."

"Delicious what in the world are you talking about this is Vanessa's house?"

"By law, Vanessa can get in to trouble because she no longer lives here and Tyrone can prove it by showing that they are in the process of getting a divorce. She is trespassing."

"Okay then Vanessa, I love you like a sister but I cannot go to jail.   I just got engaged, let's get a couple of outfits and some shoes and let's get out of here."

They are all running scared.

Delicious tells Vanessa that she can't take all those things. Tyrone will suspect something for sure, just take about four outfits and as many shoes as you can. You have so many of them that he won't notice if any of them are gone."

"Okay let's go just start grabbing the shoes, I have enough outfits to last for a couple of days, I can always buy some more things."

"Now let's get out of here please."

"Yes Vanessa, I am with Delicious."

"Okay we can go now, I have enough."

"Thank God."

"I have to get to the salon   I cannot be late. As a matter of fact I will see you later for your appointment Vanessa."

"Okay Delicious and I thank you both so much."

"Yeah girl, now it's time to get to work, I do not want to be late at all. Plus I want to show off my ring to my co-workers."

"I hear you Vikki and I love you girl. Will I see you at Desire's tonight? I will stop by for a few Vanessa, but I want to spend some time with Antonio before he leaves."

"Where is Antonio going?   You guys just got engaged."

"Antonio has to go to something called training camp and he has to leave in two days. I miss him already and he isn't gone yet."

"I understand, but this will be the perfect time for you to start looking at wedding gowns. Did you guys pick a date yet?"

"Not at all, you know that's a smart idea Vanessa. I will bring it up when I see him later, but I don't think it will be any time soon. He will probably want to get married in about two or three years."

"Two years Vikki? I really don't think it will be that long, but who knows."

"Well it was cool. I made it to work in good time, now I just need to find a parking space. Love you and I will meet you at Desire's."

"That goes double for me."

As Vanessa finishes talking to Vikki, her phone rings, it's her attorney.

"Good morning Shaunice, how are you doing today?"

"I am doing just great. Is it possible for you to come in to see me sometime this afternoon?"

"I will be finished work about four o'clock can we meet at four thirty?"

"Let me check my calendar. Okay, everything looks fine. I will see you then Vanessa."

"Until then, have a wonderful day."

Vanessa is singing. She thinks that Tyrone has agreed to the terms of the divorce and that he has signed the papers. She cannot wait to see her attorney. She is so sure that Tyrone has agreed to the terms of the divorce, she prematurely calls Vikki and tells her what is going on.

"Vikki I am so happy that Tyrone is moving forward with the divorce."

"Really that is great, I am happy for you, now you can move on with your life. I know that Kevin will be happy because he is truly in love with you and he wants to settle down with you."

"Vikki I can't wait to be with Kevin as well, he makes me happy, I have to step into a meeting in ten minutes."

"Vanessa before we hang up what time is your appointment with Delicious?"

"It's at five-thirty. Oh my goodness."

"What is it?"

"I just realized that I have to meet Shaunice at four thirty to discuss the divorce. It is not a big deal I will just have to cancel my appointment with Delicious. I am sure he will understand, once I explain it to him."

"Okay, see you always know how to make things work. Well Vanessa, please let me know what happens with Shaunice. I smell a congratulations."

"Thank you Vikki. I have five minutes to get to this meeting."

CHAPTER FIFTEEN

They both say that they love each other and hang up the phone.

Vanessa heads to her meeting, only to find out that it's been postponed to another time, Vanessa is a little ticked off, but she realizes that there is nothing she can do now, she goes back to her office and finishes typing out some contracts for her boss. The day is going by so fast. She looks up and realizes it's time to go, she heads to her attorney's office. She is excited because she is about to be divorced from Tyrone. She does not have to deal with his infidelity or him anymore. Things are great or at least Vanessa thinks it is.

Vanessa arrives at her attorney's office promptly at four thirty. She is smiling she thinks, she has a reason to celebrate. She is greeted by the receptionist.

"Hello, I am Vanessa Tyler I have a four-thirty appointment with Shaunice."

"Please have a seat Mrs. Tyler, I will let her know that you are here."

"Thank you so much."

"You are welcome. Shaunice will be with you in five minutes."

Shaunice comes out to greet Vanessa. "How are you doing today Vanessa come inside?"

"I am well Shaunice, how are you doing?"

"Well as you know, I told you that I would update you on the divorce proceedings, once I get some news."

"Yes, do not tell me. I already figured it out and you do not know how happy I am right now. I am finally going to be free from Tyrone. You are the best, Shaunice."

"Wait a minute you have to let me speak. You are getting way ahead of yourself. I just wanted to say to you that the divorce proceedings are on hold."

"On hold? What do you mean Shaunice?"

"What I am trying to say is that Tyrone does not want to get divorced. He has a change of plans and he doesn't want to sign the papers."

"Shaunice, what do you mean he doesn't want to sign the papers? How did this happen I just don't understand why he would be so mean."

"Let me ask you a question, have you spoken to Tyrone lately?"

"To be honest, yes I did, but only because I was trying to trick him into finding out when he was going to work, so that I could get the rest of my belongings out of his house. That's it."

"Well Tyrone thinks that you are interested in him and you left the door open for him to think that you have forgiven him and so he wants to put the proceedings on hold."

"What in the world? I cannot stand that man. Do you know that he had the nerve to tell me that I need to call him first before I am able to retrieve any of my clothes? He must be crazy, did he fall and hit his head on the ground, because I am not in love with him anymore, and that is the God's honest truth."

"Vanessa, I do understand what you are going through. I am going to meet with Tyrone's attorney and find out what is really going on. I will get back to you in the next couple of days. In the meantime I do not want you to have any contact with Tyrone, no phone calls, you cannot go near your home."

"But what about my clothes and shoes, my coats? I need my belongings."

"We will think of something. Is there anyone who can get the clothes for you? If so, contact them and find out if they are available and what I will do is contact Tyrone's attorney and inform him that someone will be coming to pick up your things for you. Please hang in there Vanessa, this is going to work out for the best."

"I am so sick of Tyrone and his tricks. Why is he doing this to me?"

"Tyrone is trying to get out of trying to paying alimony. But I am on to his tricks. Believe me Vanessa, he will not get out of this, you will have your divorce and he will have to pay for his indiscretions. Please go home, everything is going to be alright. Talk to you soon."

"Shaunice I just want this to be over with. I want my life back, I want to be able to love again and I cannot do that if I am still married to my creep of a husband. Every time I say my husband I get sick. I want to throw up at the mention of Tyrone's name. I need to leave. I will talk to you later. Shaunice, please pray for me. I am so mad at that man that I might do something crazy."

"Vanessa sit here. I cannot let you leave in this state of mind, is there someone that I can call for you?"

"I am okay, I can make it."

"As your attorney. you are not in the frame of mind to go home by yourself. I am going to call Vikki, since we both know her."

"Shaunice calls Vikki. Hey Vikki, this is Shaunice. How are you doing today?"

"Hey there, it has been a while since I have heard from you. Is everything okay?"

"Not really, Vanessa is sitting in my office I just gave her some news regarding her divorce. I don't think that she should drive alone, she is not in the right frame of mind. There is no telling what she might do."

"What in the world, I will be there as soon as I can. Thank you for letting me know what is going on."

"Antonio, can you please drive me to the attorney's office. Something happened with Vanessa and my friend Shaunice, who is a lawyer, called and said that Vanessa is not in the right frame of mind to drive herself home."

"What happened with Vanessa?"

"Now you know that there is such a thing as attorney client privilege. Shaunice cannot discuss anything about Vanessa's divorce with me. Vanessa will tell me herself, we will both find out soon. Will you go with me, one of us needs to drive her car?"

"Baby you got it, as much as Vanessa has done for me, I am more than happy to assist her while she is going through this divorce."

"That is why I love you so much Antonio." As they get in the car to pick up Vanessa, Vikki wants to ask Antonio about setting a date, but she is reluctant. She doesn't want him to think that she is pressuring him so soon after the engagement. "Hmm Antonio I want to ask you a question but I do not want to upset you."

"Let me hear it."

"Are you sure you won't be upset with me?"

"Vikki will you ask the question already, I am waiting."

"I will ask you but you have to promise me that you will not yell at me."

"Vikki I promise, scout's honor."

Vikki smiles, but tells Antonio, "when we get back home, can we sit down and pick a date for our wedding? I know that we won't be able to get married for at least two years."

"Okay, why would I be mad? We can discuss it when we get back home, and for the record I am not mad at all honey, you can always talk to me about any and everything."

Antonio and Vikki finally arrive at the attorney's office. They both notice that Vanessa has been crying.

Vikki asks Shaunice what happened.

She explains that she cannot discuss the divorce, but that the proceedings have taken a major turn.

"She might not tell you, but I am going to say it. That butt hole jerk of a husband of mine decided to retract the divorce papers."

"What are you saying Vanessa? What I am saying Vikki, is that Tyrone decided that he does not want to get a divorce."

"Vanessa, are you kidding me?"

"No Vikki, I am not kidding, this is no time to joke."

"That is crazy because Tyrone was so in love with Kayla and he wanted them to be together and to raise their child as a family. And all of a sudden he does not want to be with Kayla, there has got to more to it than meets the eye."

"There is more to it. Tyrone is still in love with Vanessa and he wants to fight to get her back."

"Whoa run that by me again Shaunice."

"Tyrone is still in love with "who?" Now that is funny, my friend did everything she could to make him happy and he stepped on her heart because she couldn't have his children. Tyrone needs help. Let me behave before I say something that I shouldn't say."

Antonio is surprised by Tyrone's actions. "Wow Tyrone is truly unbelievable. Vanessa I am so sorry, you know that Vikki and I will always have your back. So what is the next step?"

Shaunice replies, "Vikki, you said something earlier that I did not remember before and it might be the one thing that might make Tyrone continue with the divorce."

"I did? I cannot remember what I said earlier."

"You said that that the woman Tyrone cheated on Vanessa with is pregnant. That is my ammunition, I am almost sure that Tyrone does not want his coworkers to know anything about that."

"You guys take Vanessa home and just be there for her. Vanessa this changes things. I will call you in a few days, and remember there is to be no contact with Tyrone at all; and that includes you two. Stay away from Tyrone. Do I make myself clear?"

They all say in unison "yes" to Shaunice.

"Now please go home and relax, tomorrow is a new day."

"Thanks again Shaunice."

"You are very welcome, Vanessa."

Vikki gets into Vanessa's car. She is going to drive, despite the conversation that they just had with Shaunice. Vanessa is still in no frame of mind to drive anywhere.

"Vikki, I could kill Tyrone right now. He has the nerve to pretend that he is still in love with me, so that he won't have to pay alimony. I didn't think that I could hate anyone, but Tyrone is at the top of the list."

"Vanessa, now you know you don't hate Tyrone. You just aren't feeling him right now, and please tell me that you did not just say that you want to shoot him."

"No I didn't say that I wanted to shoot him, I said that I want to kill him, and yes I meant every word of it too. The only thing that is stopping me is that I would hurt so many people, including his unborn child."

"Why are you so concerned about his child? He got someone else pregnant and you are concerned about that kid."

"Vikki, you know that is not fair. That child does not have anything to do with this, it is not the baby's fault that Tyrone is in this type of situation. What would that teach the child? Nothing at all."

"The best thing for me to do is stay away from him and let God handle this whole situation. I want to go home and relax I am going to call Kevin. I need him."

"As Vanessa is trying to say Kevin's name, she burst into tears again."

He is yelling on the other end of the phone. "Vanessa baby, what is wrong?"

It is hard for her to get anything out through all the tears. Vikki has to stop and put her blue tooth on so that she can speak to Kevin.

"Kevin this is Vikki. Look, can you come to Vanessa's house when you get off of work?"

"I am already off. I am on my way."

"I will explain everything to you when you get there."

"Okay then, I will see you there soon."

"Okay. Thank you."

"There is no need to thank me, you know that I would do anything for Vanessa. I plan on making her my wife one day."

"That is good to know. Be blessed."

"Vanessa, Kevin is going to stop by your house he is going to keep you company. Is that okay?"

"Yeah girl, it is perfectly okay."

Vanessa is so hurt by Tyrone's actions that she sleeps all the way on the ride home.

"Vanessa, we're here."

"Here where?"

"Girl at your house, are you sure you are okay?"

"Yeah, I am fine."

"No you are not. Antonio and I will stay with you until Kevin arrives. Come on in the house now."

"Antonio baby, can you get something out of the refrigerator so I can cook something to for us to eat?"

"Hey baby there is a nice Italian restaurant a few blocks away I will jump in the car and get something to eat for all of us."

"Okay honey just be sure to get enough for four people."

"Four people? Honey, there are only three of us here."

"Kevin is on his way."

"Cool, we can chit chat while you talk to Vanessa."

"Antonio, please go get some food. I just want to make sure that Vanessa eats, this has been a trying day for her and I don't want her to be sick."

"I'm going."

"Thanks, love you baby."

Vikki helps Vanessa take off her shoes. She escorts her to the sofa and tells her to lie down. She goes into the kitchen and makes a cup of tea for the both of them. This will give them time to talk for a few moments without anyone else around.

"Sista, it is going to be okay. I believe that Tyrone will come to his senses and not contest the divorce any longer. I am so surprised at him, now he wants to pretend that he is in love with you and wants to start over, all because he doesn't want to give you any money."

"Vikki, I don't understand why he would torment me like this." Just as she says this to Vanessa her phone rings. She goes to answer it but when she looks at the number she is shocked to see that it is Tyrone who is calling her. "Oh my goodness Vikki, it's Tyrone calling me."

"Why in the world is he calling you? There is something fishy about this whole situation. Do not answer the call you heard what your lawyer told you this evening."

"I'm not answering him."

Since Tyrone cannot seem to get Vanessa on the phone he decides to text her. Now she wants to know who is texting her. She looks at her phone, she has just received a text message from Tyrone. What now? He asks her if she stopped by the house because some of her things were moved. Vanessa wants to respond, but she knows that she can't, so she does her best to ignore him. The doorbell rings.

"I will get the door Vanessa, you just relax it's probably Antonio back with the food."

"Vanessa he couldn't possibly be back that fast with the food."

Vikki looks through the peephole and she notices that it is not Antonio, it is actually Kevin. She opens the door and invites him in. They give each other a hug. "How are you Kevin? It is good to see you."

"The same here Vikki. Now what's going on with my girl?"

"Kevin, I think that is something that she should tell you herself."

Vikki escorts Kevin to the living room. To both of their surprise, Vanessa is watching television.

Kevin kisses Vanessa. They hug and kiss each other like they are in a relationship. "Baby what happened? Just know this that whatever it is that you are going through, remember that I am here to go through it with you, you are not alone. And although we are not officially together we are still one."

"Kevin you always seem to know the right things to say at the right time. I went to see my attorney today she wanted to update me on the divorce proceedings. It seems as though Tyrone has decided to contest the divorce."

"Why is he contesting the divorce?"

"It seems that Tyrone is still in love with me and that he realizes that he messed up and he wants to fight to keep the marriage together."

"What did you say?"

"Kevin what do you think I said. I am no longer in love with him and I am mad as hell that he is trying to contest this divorce when he was the one who cheated on me. The bottom line is that he doesn't want to pay alimony, so he will find the slightest thing to not file the papers, but all that will be taken care of."

"Well he needs to sign the papers. Vanessa, do you need me to talk to him for you?"

"No, I am not supposed to have any contact with him and no one in my circle is supposed to have any contact with him." As she is about to finish her conversation the bell rings. "Who is it?"

"It's Antonio."

"Vikki, can you please let your husband in."

"I sure can." Vikki opens the door. "Honey, let me help you with that, this food sure smells good."

"I hear a man's voice in the living room what is that about?"

"That is Kevin."

"Let me go and say hello to Kevin. My main man Kevin, how are you doing?   Brother it is certainly good to see you."

They slap each other five. "Brother it is good to see you."

"Vanessa is like family, treat her right."

"Now you know I got this. I not only love this woman, but I am in love with her. I would never do anything to hurt her. I want to love her the way she should be loved."

"So I guess she told you about Tyrone?"

"Yeah man, she filled me in on it. I'm a little pissed right now. What makes that Negro think that she is going back to him? He has lost his mind. I am almost tempted to go over there and knock his block off."

"Kevin he is not worth it. I cannot have any contact with him and neither can you, so whatever you want to do get it out of your mind."

"I just want to talk to him."

"Kevin did you hear what I said? Sweetheart, you cannot have any contact with Tyrone. If you do that, it will make the divorce proceedings longer and we do not want that. Plus my attorney told me that she has a way to get Tyrone to sign the papers sooner."

"And what is that Vanessa?"

"Well she forgot that Tyrone's mistress is pregnant with his child. My attorney said that will make my case stronger because Tyrone doesn't want any problems, especially since he just made partner in his firm, so I am sure that he will not contest the divorce after that; but who knows what Tyrone will do. I just hope that he signs the papers. I want him out of my life for good."

"Vanessa stop getting all yourself worked up about Tyrone, things will work out. Now I have some news."

"What is that Vikki?"

"Antonio and I have decided to set a date for our wedding and I need your input, since you are going to be my maid of honor. I say that we can get married in two years. Do you think that is too soon Antonio?"

"I think that is too long; that's what I wanted to talk to you about. I am leaving in two months for training camp, and I won't be back home until after the football season is over. I don't want to wait too long, so I was thinking that we could get married the beginning of August. It will be before training camp. I don't want to wait to make you Mrs. Antonio Anderson. How do you feel about that Vikki?"

Vikki is shelled shocked, she can't get anything out. She can't do anything but cry.

"What's wrong baby?"

Talking through her tears Vikki tells Antonio that she is so happy. I never thought that I would find someone who would really love me for me, this is the best day of my life. "Antonio I would marry you at City Hall, if I could."

"So let's do it."

"Antonio you would get me killed by all my family and friends. This is going to be my one and only wedding and I want to do it right. I don't want a huge wedding party, but I do want to walk down the aisle with a wedding gown with the man of my dreams. Is that okay?"

"Baby, whatever you want."

"Great, I have exactly six weeks to plan a wedding."

"Kevin, would you be one of my groomsmen?"

"Antonio man, it would be my honor. Vikki is a great woman. I am so happy for the both of you."

"Hey guys, can we eat, I have had a trying day. I haven't eaten all day and I am getting sick. I'm with you Vanessa, let's eat before this food gets cold. And when we finish, can you two please leave so Vanessa and I can look at wedding dresses."

"Vikki I'm not leaving without you. Honey it is getting late and I don't want you driving alone late at night. Maybe you and Vanessa can do that another time."

"Antonio you are so right I didn't realize the time. Well I want to thank you, Vanessa, for tonight. It was great food and great company, but I do have to go to work in the morning."

"After we are married I don't want you working like that Vikki. You are the wife of a professional athlete. I don't know about my teammates, but I want my wife to stay at home. And if she wants to go on the road with me sometimes, then that's her choice, but she won't have to work at all."

"Antonio that's so sweet, but I'm so used to working I wouldn't feel right not working. Honey, we will discuss that at another time."

"Okay Mr. Anderson, now give me a kiss and let's go and let the other two love birds be alone."

Kevin asks Vanessa in a sexy voice, "Baby do you need me to stay?"

"No Kevin, I actually feel better. Kevin promise me that you won't go anywhere near Tyrone. After the divorce, you can do whatever you want."

"Baby I double promise you. No contact, until after the divorce."

"And Antonio and I promise not to flatten his tires until the divorce is final." They all chuckle.

"Good night I love the three of you. Vikki, I will see you tomorrow I have to see Delicious."

"Okay girl, see you tomorrow."

"Love and Peace."

"Okay what am I going to do now? Everyone is gone. I know, I know this is crazy, but something is telling me to check on Kayla. I will call her now. I hope it's not too late to call her."

"Hello Kayla, this is Vanessa Tyler, are you sleeping?"

"Hi Vanessa, it is perfectly okay. How are you doing?"

"I am okay. I just called to see how you were doing?"

"I cannot believe that after everything that went down between me and Tyrone that you would continue to communicate with me."

"Kayla, I am not a mean person and you are carrying his child, and in some sort of way I feel attached to the baby. I don't want to keep you on the phone too long, just wanted to make sure that you are okay."

"Thank you for calling. We are thankful for that."

"We, so there is someone special in your life?"

"Yes there is, but we will talk about that some other time."

"Well, good for you. I am happy for the two of you."

"Once again, I am sorry for calling so late, you take care."

Vanessa hangs up the phone with Kayla.

Tyrone is at Kayla's place. Kayla has agreed to talk to Tyrone. Her feelings have totally changed about him, but Tyrone is definitely not one to give up. When he wants something, he will step on anyone who gets in his way. Well this time he has another thing coming.

"Why was Vanessa calling you?"

"She just wanted to check on me and see how I am doing. What business is it of yours? You are not with her anymore."

"I am just surprised that she would contact you."

"Tyrone, your soon to be ex-wife is not a bad person. I actually got the chance to sit down and talk to her. She is a rather nice person. After speaking to her, I felt guilty that I cheated with you."

"Did she mention me?"

"Why in the world would she mention you? Oh so I guess you don't know?"

"What in the world are you talking about Tyrone?"

"Well, I am contesting the divorce."

"Tyrone why would you do that? I thought you said that you don't love her anymore."

"I don't love Vanessa, but the only way I won't have to give up my money is if she cheats on me."

"Tyrone that is dumb, how can she cheat on you and you two are getting a divorce?"

"Well I pretended that I am still in love with her and I wanted to work things out with her so that I can catch her with someone else; and that will be my reason for not having to pay her. I can say that she is in a relationship with someone else, and that she cheated on me; and even though we are getting a divorce, we were still legally married."

"I think it's a good plan."

"Please Tyrone, I know you don't think that Vanessa is going to fall for that garbage."

"You don't know Vanessa that well, she will come back to me soon, just give it some time. We were married for twelve years, it is hard to walk away from that and walk away from me."

"Tyrone don't be so sure of yourself this time why don't you leave her alone and let her live her life. And it is these childish types of games that you play why I cannot be bothered with you either. Can you do me a real big favor?"

"I will do anything for you Kayla, just let me know what it is."

"Can you please leave? Go home, I am tired and right now I am tired of you."

"I beg your pardon. I don't tolerate that type of disrespect."

"Tyrone who disrespected you" I am tired of you. I am pregnant and there are going to be times when I do not feel like being bothered with anyone; so with that being said, can you please go home to your nice empty home."

"Tyrone is highly upset with Kayla, but there is nothing that he can do but listen to her and leave; after all he still thinks the baby she is carrying is actually his."

"Kayla, the only reason that I am leaving is because you are pregnant and I don't want anything to stress you out. I will be back tomorrow."

"Tyrone, please call before you come."

"What do you mean that I have to call before I come over here?"

"Tyrone I think I speak very clear English. You cannot show up at my house and think that it is okay. I might not be in the mood to be bothered with you tomorrow. Like I said, call before you come over. Now please leave."

Tyrone slams the door. "I am out of here, believe that. I will talk to you when you are in a better mood."

Kayla mumbles under her breath. "I will be in a better mood when you leave."

"Kayla what was that smart remark?"

"Good night Tyrone."

"Yeah, whatever Kayla."

I thought he would never leave. I have to sit down for a minute he always stresses me out and that's not good for me or the baby. I need to call Michael and remind him about my doctor's appointment.

"Hey Michael baby, where are you?"

"Honey I am still at the office, still finishing this meeting."

"This late? Yes remember the company MacGrubber and Associates? They finally agreed to our terms. I am drained, this was a marathon meeting. I am wrapping it up. I should be there shortly."

"Okay then I can wait until you get here to remind you about tomorrow."

"Tomorrow, what's happening tomorrow?"

"Michael, it's not that important; we can talk about it when you come home."

"Kayla are you sure?"

"Michael will you finish up the meeting. I love you I'll see you when you get here."

"Okay, I love you too."

God I love that man so much please let this baby be his. It will break his heart if this baby doesn't belong to him. I won't think negatively I am positive this is Michael's baby. It has got to be. Okay Kayla stop stressing yourself over something you have no control. Michael and I will cross that bridge when the time comes.

Kayla hears Michael pull up in his car she is wondering how he finished the meeting and got back home so fast. He must have driven like a bat out of hell.

"Michael baby, how in the world did you get here so fast?"

"I just found another way to come home; it saves so much time and I don't have to fight with traffic. How is my favorite lady doing?"

"I am much better now that you are here."

"Are you okay, is the baby okay?"

"Yes Michael, we are both fine. I was a little dizzy earlier, so I had to lie down and I am feeling better now."

"That is wonderful, now what did you want to remind me about tomorrow?"

"I have a doctor's appointment tomorrow and I wanted to make sure that you were still going to take me."

"Not only will I take you, but I want to stay with you while you go through all of your tests. I cleared my calendar for tomorrow, all my meetings have been canceled."

"Michael, you didn't have to do that."

"I know that I didn't have to do that. I did it because I wanted to spend time with my future wife and my baby."

"I love you so much Michael. You are incredible."

"I feel the same way about you baby. Now can we get some rest? I am tired."

"You must be tired because you don't want to eat, nor did you tell me how the meeting turned out."

"Short version, the meeting was a success and I ate at the office."
Michael kisses Kayla on her forehead.
"Good night handsome."
"Good night gorgeous."

CHAPTER SIXTEEN

It's a calm Thursday morning. The sun is shining brightly. It is a hot and humid summer day. Kayla is preparing to see her doctor today. She prays quietly that the baby is healthy and that everything turns out okay. She is excited because she finally gets to spend some quality time with Michael.

Michael is already up and almost dressed to go with Kayla. He is more excited than Kayla is because this will be his first child. "Come on baby, I don't want us to be late."

"Michael I am coming as fast as I can. I will be downstairs in about three minutes."

"Okay, I will be in the car waiting for you."

"Alright, take this bag for me please."

"Okay, but let's go."

"Michael, you act as though you are the one getting examined."

"I can't finish getting dressed if you are going to keep talking. Now go get in the car."

Kayla doesn't want to alarm Michael but she is not feeling too good. She waits until he leaves to sit down for a breather. She doesn't understand what's wrong.

Michael heads downstairs and gets in the car to start it up, he is waiting for Kayla to come downstairs. *I know it's only been a minute, but I thought she would be walking out the door. I will give her a minute more.* Michael is upset that Kayla has not come downstairs yet, *what in the world is that woman doing?* He calls her cell phone but she is not answering, *let me go back inside and get her.* Michael gets out of his car and proceeds to go back into the house. He is calling out to Kayla, but she is not responding, *where can she be?* Michael runs upstairs, thinking that Kayla might be in the restroom. Michael is shocked by what he sees, Kayla is on the floor. " Oh my goodness. Kayla baby wake up." Michael is shaken, he immediately calls the police. He is so confused he forgets where he lives, he just wants them to come quickly.

The operator tells Michael that he must get his bearings, so that they can get there as soon as possible. Michael does exactly what he is told to do, he calms down enough to give them pertinent information. The paramedics are there within minutes.

"Help me, I am up here in the bedroom." They rush upstairs and shove Michael out of the way. "Help her please. Is she okay?"

"Sir you have to move out of the way so we can examine her."

"Please let her be okay."

"What happened here?"

"We were both getting ready to go see her doctor. Look man, are they going to be okay?"

"They who?"

"Her and the baby, she is pregnant with my child."

"Sir please move back, let us get her out of here."

"Where are you taking to her?"

"Where does her primary doctor work?"

"She is at Mercy General."

"Sir please let us do our job, meet us at the hospital. In case of emergency who should we contact?"

"Does she have a family member that we can call?"

Michael informs EMS that Kayla doesn't have any family members who are listed as an emergency contact. I am the person who would be the emergency contact.

"Okay I need you to answer some questions. Does she have high blood pressure?"

"Definitely not, she doesn't have any diseases she is in perfect health."

"Is she going to be alright you haven't told me anything?"

"Sir we have to get moving. We need to get her to the hospital as quick as possible. Please let us do our job, we are going to assist her the best way we can."

"Is it okay if I ride in my car?"

"Sure you can sir."

"I am coming right now." As Michael is driving he starts to pray.

Michael is crying hysterically. The woman of his dreams is being rushed to the hospital. *I need to pray right now.* "Lord I don't know what happened to my fiancée please take care of her and heal her body. I believe that you can do it Lord."

Michael is pacing back and forth, he doesn't know what's going on. At that moment, the doctors come and speak with him.

"How Kayla is doing?"

"She is going to be ok, she needs plenty of rest and she has to stay off her feet for a few days."

"How long will she be here?"

"She can go home in a day or two."

"Thank God. Can I see her? Not now she is sleeping."

Kayla is finally out of the hospital. She is home resting, but she is not the type to sit home and do nothing. She needs to keep busy, she is stubborn as they come. She calls Michael, "Hey baby, I just wanted to see how the meeting was going. Do you need me to come in?"

"Kayla are you crazy, you're on bed rest. I can handle things here. Good bye love you, I'll call when I have a free moment."

That man gets me so mad at times, but I love him. She decides to call her attorney she needs to speak to her about getting child support as soon as the baby is born. "Hello Brittany how are you doing? I need to see you. Is it possible to come in today?"

"Sure I'm free. Can you get here about ten o'clock?"

"Yes that will be fine. Thank you."

Kayla arrives at her attorney's office/ she explains that she wants to file child support papers against her child's father. She tells her attorney that she had an affair with him and now she's pregnant and he doesn't want anything to do with her and the baby. His name is Tyrone Tyler. He is a Partner with an Investment Brokerage Firm, he makes close to five million dollars a year.

Her attorney tells her that she will file the papers immediately.

"That's it Kayla, I will call you when you need to appear in court. I'm going to call you in a few a days."

Tyrone will wish he never treated me the way he has. Let me get home before Michael gets back. If he knew I went out, he would have a tantrum. Kayla leaves her attorney and heads home. She is driving fast, but not too fast, she doesn't want to get stopped for a ticket. She made it home okay. As soon as she gets home, Michael calls to say that he is coming home for a couple of hours to be with her. Kayla says out loud "how close was that"? Here comes Michael now.

"Kayla baby are you here?"

"Yes Michael where else would I be?"

"I have to watch out for you because you don't like to listen. How do you feel?"

"I feel better I'm just a little hungry that's all."

"Okay I will run downstairs and whip up something for you to eat, one cheese omelet on the way."

"Michael this tastes so good I should make you cook all the time." Kayla and Michael both share a good laugh.

Michael tells Kayla that he has to get back to work for another meeting he has, but that he loves her and he will be back later tonight. They give each other a kiss.

"See you honey and I want you to rest."

"Okay, I promise." Kayla has no other choice, but to do what the doctor tells her. She doesn't want to lose Michael's baby. Kayla drifts off to sleep, she doesn't hear anything, her phone is ringing like crazy. Michael is a worry wart he begins to panic, as usual. He rushes from work only to find that Kayla is knocked out, she doesn't even know that he was there. She is so tired that she slept through the night. Michael slept on the couch just so he wouldn't awaken her.

The next morning Kayla receives a phone call from her attorney. She tells Kayla that she has a date on the calendar regarding her child support.

"Brittany, how did you do that so fast?"

"Truth be told he already has a case and when I found out I added this case to it."

"So Brittany, when are we going to court?"

"We have to appear in two days. Kayla beware, he is going to fight this."

"I don't care, whatever it takes."

"Okay you take care, see you on Wednesday at three o'clock part three. Have a wonderful day."

"Thank you and I will." Kayla calls her doctor. She wants to go out, she is tired of being stuck in the house. "Hello Dr. Jackson how are you? This is Kayla Jones."

"How are you Kayla?"

"I'm okay, I'm calling because I would like to go out I'm sick of being here. I won't do anything to harm the baby. Can I go to the gym or go shopping?"

"Only if you won't be doing anything that is strenuous."

"Dr. Jackson, I promise that I won't." She hangs up and says yes, she is so loud that she wakes Michael. "I'm sorry baby but I just got some great news."

"What great news did you get?"

"The doctor just cleared me to go out as long as I don't do anything strenuous. I am so happy now I can go for my morning walks again."

"Kayla baby, are you sure?"

"Yes I'm sure, Michael you have to stop worrying so much. I won't do anything to harm me or the baby I promise. I love you baby. I'll see you when I come back from my walk."

"Okay, and don't push yourself. Love you."

To Kayla's surprise Michael isn't around, *that's funny I thought he would be here when I got back from my walk.* She calls him on the phone. "Hey honey where are you?"

I'm at work, you're right Kayla. I need to have faith, so I decided not to be my normal pain in the butt."

Kayla lovingly says, "Remember you said it, I didn't. Okay honey have a great day."

"Okay let me go I have to close this deal."

"I'm not worried, I know you can do it. Love you."

"Ditto girl. Smooches."

What should I do next? I know what. I have to call Delicious for an appointment. "Hey Delicious, this is Kayla. Is it possible for you to do my hair? Let me see what I have available. I can fit you in tomorrow afternoon is three o'clock okay for you."

"That's perfect I will be there, see you then."

"Okay see you tomorrow, have a good day."

"The same to you Delicious."

"Okay who is this calling me? It must be important, they were calling me while I was talking to Delicious."

"Hello this is Kayla, how may I help you?"

"Hello Kayla, this is Brittany, your attorney. I was wondering can you be in court tomorrow at twelve o'clock noon."

"Is this about my case?"

"Yes it is."

"Brittany, that was fast."

"After meeting with Mr. Tyler and his attorney I don't think he wanted to prolong this too much longer. See you tomorrow."

"See you tomorrow and thank you Brittany."

"Don't thank me just yet. We still have to get a ruling from the judge. You will be fine, no matter what the outcome is."

"Yes, I will be okay have a great day."

"Thank you Kayla and you have a great day as well."

Kayla is excited because she won't have to fight with Tyrone about the child support. This is his baby and he should take care of it. *Boy this phone is busy today, now who is this?*

It's Michael. *I think I should call him back before he panics.* "Hey handsome how are you?"

"I'm good, just checking in."

"I am great, you're at work late again Michael. I'm feeling like you don't want to be bothered with me now that I am pregnant. If you don't want me or the baby, let me know. I will start looking for a place to go."

"Kayla what are you talking about? I'm not avoiding you. I'm just trying to make money for us, so when the baby comes, you don't have to work as hard. I just finished meeting with some potential clients, I think we wooed them. I'm on my way home do you need anything?"

"Actually I don't want anything I just want to get some rest. I have an appointment to get my hair done tomorrow at three o'clock and Lord knows I need it."

"Baby you ain't never lied. Michael is smiling as he says that. I'll see you when I get home that's only if you're not sleep."

"I will try and wait up for you, but I can't promise you that."

"I understand. See you when you get home."

CHAPTER SEVENTEEN

It's a nice cool Wednesday morning. Vanessa is up preparing to go to work. She is wondering who is calling her so early in the morning. It turns out that it's Shaunie, her attorney.

"Good morning Shaunie, how do you do?"

"I am good Vanessa, I have some good news."

"You do?"

"Yes, it seems that Tyrone wants to settle, so I need you to be in court today at twelve o'clock noon. Is that okay with you?"

"That's a perfect time, it works out because I don't have school today."

"Okay, I will see you at twelve o'clock noon." Vanessa can't wait to tell Vikki the good news. She calls Vikki. "Guess what Vikki, Tyrone has agreed to settle.   This mean the divorce is going to go through. I am so happy."

"Vanessa that is such great news and I am truly happy for you. You deserve happiness in your life."

Vikki, thank you for always having my back. I really do appreciate you."

"Girl, you know I love you."

"I'm so sorry, how are the wedding plans going?"

"I haven't been much of a maid of honor, you know with school and work. It's been kind of hectic for me, but I get a break soon and I will help you with whatever you need."

"Thank you Vanessa. I appreciate that, and I need you to try on your dress."

"Okay, you just tell me when. I have got to go. I want to call Kevin and let him know what's going on. Meet me at Desire's at three o'clock, I am going to treat you."

"You're going to treat me?"

"Yes Vikki, you can get whatever you want done to your hair and I will pay for it."

"You don't have to do that Vanessa."

"I know that I don't have to do it. I want to do it and I will not take no for an answer."

"Okay, you win."

"Later girl, I have to go. Now let me call Kevin. Is this that handsome man of mine Kevin?"

"Only if your name is Vanessa Tyler."

"Well this is Vanessa, but I won't be a Tyler too much longer. Tyrone decided not to contest the divorce any longer, and I can't be happier."

"Vanessa baby, we can celebrate tomorrow. I can't wait for us to be together officially, no more sneaking around like we are common criminals."

"Kevin, I agree one hundred ten percent, now I can show everyone my new man. Yes this is great. Well it's time for me to go to work I will speak to you when I get to work."

"Okay baby."

"Have a great day Kevin. And Kevin, I love you, thank you for being part of my life."

Vanessa goes to work and is so excited about her court date that she forgot to call Delicious to make an appointment with him. *Let me do that now before I forget.* She starts to call Delicious. Please pick up… thank God. "Delicious, this is Vanessa. I forgot to call you to make an appointment for today."

"Now Vanessa, you are my best customer. You don't need an appointment, any time you want to come in today, you can."

"Well I have to be in court at twelve o'clock noon."

"What happened girl?"

"Nothing, Tyrone decided not to contest the divorce anymore."

"Sista Girl, that is great news! Then I will see you afterwards."

"You got it."

Vanessa is so giddy at work. She is doing everything so that she can leave earlier than usual. All the typing and meetings have been scheduled. She has done so much that it seems like she has been there all day. *Boy how time flies, it's already eleven a.m.* She needs to start wrapping up her work so that she can head to court.

Vanessa arrives to court at exactly twelve she is happy with excitement. Just as Vanessa arrives, Shaunice walks through the door; they hug each other. They enter the courtroom. Tyrone is there with his attorney also. They all rise as the judge comes in, everyone sits as they are ordered to do.

Everyone is nervous about what the judge is going to say. No one knows who she is going to rule in favor of.

The judge is going back and forth with the attorneys, trying to hash things out.

Tyrone doesn't want to be there, but he has no choice. After about twenty minutes the judge makes her ruling. She actually rules in Vanessa's favor. The divorce has been granted, now all each of them has to do is sign the papers.

Both Vanessa and Tyrone are happy that the divorce is over. The judge tells both of them that she will make her final decision on what the settlement will be by close of business, next day. Both of them agree.

Vanessa is so happy that her divorce is final that she walks out of the courtroom, skipping like a little kid; and she barely sees Vikki and Kevin. "It's over you guys. I'm free and single and I am so happy. Thank God."

"Thank you Shaunice, for all of your help… it was well worth it."

"You're welcome, it's not final until the judge signs off on the settlement portion tomorrow. Shaunice, I really don't care about that. I'm just glad that I am no longer married to that man. Okay, let's get out of here. We have to go and get dolled up."

"Baby, I wish I could stay, but I have to get back to work. I will meet you at the salon when I get off."

"Okay baby, now give me a kiss Kevin."

"Now that's what I'm talking about. Bring those lips over here."

"Baby, now let me go and get cute for our celebration dinner later tonight."

"Okay, I'm outta here."

"Vanessa, let's go and get fabulous so we can go and enjoy ourselves tonight, with those incredible men of ours."

"Let's go Vanessa, you know how Delicious gets if we're late."

"Yeah he gets extra." Both of them laugh.

As they leave the courthouse, they see Kayla from a distance. The women want to know what she is there for. And of course you know Vikki asks her.

"Hello Kayla, what brings you this way?"

"Well I have some personal business to take care of."

"Oh really, you do?"

"Yes, I really do."

"Well, I hope and pray that everything works out for you. Nice running into you."

"Vanessa, now you know what she came here for. I bet she is trying to get child support from Tyrone."

"Well, if she does, then good for her; she should do what she feels is best for her. Don't mean to sound selfish, but right now I'm concerned about me. God will work it out for her."

"Here comes Delicious."

"What! You ladies are here and on time. I don't believe it, you know you can always go straight to the back. Now go have a seat and wait for me, I'll be back in about three minutes."

"Vanessa you seem a little too giddy, we will talk when I come back." As Delicious returns from the reception area, he starts doing Vikki's hair.

"Okay Vanessa, what's with the glow girl? I see it all over you. You are cheesing too much."

"I just got some great news."

"Well, what is it?"

"I'm Free."

"Okay, you're free. What's so good about that?"

"I'm free, as in my divorce is final."

"What! Are you for real?"

"Thank you Jesus, girl I am so happy for you. You deserve some happiness in your life."

Vanessa's phone rings, it's Shaunice on the other line. "Hello Shaunice, did something happen?"

"Yes, the judge ruled on your divorce settlement today."

"She did? What did she say?"

"I just wanted to let you know what you are getting." Shaunice tells Vanessa the dollar amount that she received from the divorce and what Tyrone has to fork up. "And he must pay my attorney fees."

"Are you kidding me? Thank you for getting back to me I appreciate that."

"Vanessa, what did she say?"

"Shaunice said that the judge awarded me $20.5 million dollars, 2 cars, the vacation home and $150,000 a month on top of the $20.5 million for pain and suffering."

Vikki says to Vanessa, "I told you Tyrone was going to get what was coming to him." Just as she says that Tyrone comes to the shop.

"What are you doing here?"

"I just wanted to get my keys from you, the locks have been changed and if you haven't gotten you things out by now, then please call and I will make arrangements for you to get them. You can keep the car, I don't want it."

"That's funny, you are telling me that I can keep the car? Baby you can have your car because the divorce settlement just came back."

"It came back already?"

"Yes it did, and it didn't take long for the judge to rule in my favor at all. Thank you for hurting me Tyrone, although I'm still hurt this $20.5 million dollars helps ease the pain a whole lot."

Just as Vanessa says that to Tyrone, guess who comes walking into Desire's Hair Salon? You guessed right. Kayla.

"Kayla, what are you doing here?"

"Tyrone, I've been looking for you everywhere. I wanted to hand this to you personally."

"What is this?"

"These are child support papers."

Here's the catch: Kayla found out that Tyrone is not the father of her baby, but she has been awarded child support anyway, she is making him pay for the way he treated her.

"What! Child Support are you kidding me? Woman I know you are joking."

"Yes Tyrone, child support and I'm not kidding; and that's how much you have to pay each month, $50,000 a month from the ages of birth until 3 years old, and once the baby turns 4 you must pay me $100,000 a month until the child turns 18 years of age."

"Are you crazy? The baby isn't even born yet."

"Well that's what the judge decided, weren't you in court?"

"Yes, but I didn't know that they made that decision; I had to leave before the decision was made. That is some crap I'm paying for a baby that isn't born, be glad this is my child you are carrying." Just as Tyrone says that to Kayla, Michael walks in and hears this.

"Kayla is this true? Does that baby you're carrying belong to Tyrone, and not me? I'm waiting for an answer."

"Well Michael, you see…"

"Well, hell! I see alright, you know what! I am done with you. I trusted you and this is what I get. Go and be with your baby daddy."

"Michael, please don't leave, let me explain it to you." Kayla walks out of the shop behind Michael.

"Well Tyrone, you know the saying?"

"Delicious, I really don't know what you are talking about at all."

"Let me see, you cheat on your wife for five years; so you have to pay alimony, and to top it off you get someone else pregnant, and now you have to pay child support." Before he can finish …

Michael and Kayla both enter the shop again, after Michael has found out some shocking news. "Kayla, I want you to tell Tyrone what you just told me."

"This is not the place, I'm not sure that I should say anything here in front of everyone."

"Tell him now."

"Michael, I don't want to do this here. I think there has been enough embarrassment for one day. I don't want to hurt him anymore."

"Let me say it again, tell him now! Right now!!"

Kayla hesitantly tells Tyrone the baby she's carrying is not his. "Tyrone, you are paying child support for a kid that doesn't belong to you."

"What! Now I know you are lying."

"Here's the proof, the proof is in the pudding."

"What! How is that, I have never heard of anything like this. How can you determine who the baby's father is and the baby isn't born?"

"Modern Technology, it's the best."

Delicious wants to talk and he says he wants to finish what he was saying. "Like I was trying to say before I was interrupted, you know the old saying. DON'T PLAY IF YOU CAN'T PAY."

Tyrone is upset. He can't believe his eyes or that a judge would make him pay child support for a baby that is not his. All he can say is "I'll be damn!"

Vikki says loudly, "I'm leaving!" This is just way too much for me to handle right now. I've got a man to get home to."

Vanessa chimes in. "I'm right behind you, and Tyrone I'm sorry that it had to end this way."

"Wait Vanessa, do you think that we can try and make this thing work?"

"Tyrone I don't think we can try; I know we can't try. It's not going to work, so please go about your business. That's what happens when you play, you have to pay."

"I've got a man at home; and by the way Tyrone, not only are we getting married soon, we are also having a baby."

"But Vanessa, that's impossible."

"Tyrone, with God all things are possible, and it wasn't that I couldn't have kids; all the stress you put me through wouldn't allow me to have kids, so enjoy yourself."

Delicious says seductively, "Well Tyrone, are you ready to come over to the other side? I'm ready to recycle. Hey if you pay me, you can sure play with me… now that's funny."

"Delicious go somewhere with your foolishness. I'm in no mood to be bothered."

"Tyrone, I am here if you ever need to talk."

"Good night and good-bye Delicious."

ABOUT THE AUTHOR

This is Sharyn's second book, but her first Romance Novel.

She is a disciple of the East Ward Missionary Baptist Church.

Sharyn is single and currently resides in New York City.

9 780692 406878